The Brothers

The Brothers

by
Ian Lennox

Gordon Liberty Publishing

ISBN 0-9546359-1-4

Design and typesetting by www.simprimstudio.com

Printed and bound in Great Britain by
Martins the Printers Limited, Sea View Works, Spittal, Berwick-upon-Tweed
www.martins-the-printers.com

Published by Gordon Liberty Publishing in 2005
© Ian Lennox 2005

The author asserts his moral right to be identified as the
author of this work.

All rights reserved.
No part of this publication may be reproduced,
stored in a retrieval system, or transmitted, in any form
or by any means, electronic, mechanical, photocopying, recording or
otherwise, without the prior permission of the publisher.

FOREWARD

The Brothers is a fascinating story which draws you into their compulsive, intricate, and dangerous lives.

Set against the background of The Great War, Ian Lennox's flair for reality illuminates a stark insight into two young men's journeys as they both go their incredible, but uncertain, separate ways. On each page you can almost taste the impact they have on family and community.

The research and exposition is flawless whilst the narrative drives you on relentlessly with each heartbeat- and takes no prisoners.

This is a smashing read.

Arthur McKenzie Sept 2005

Author's Note
While the story is clearly set in Northumberland for reason of plot geography and topography I have created the village of Milford and a giant forest of beech trees.

Thanks
A big thank-you for all your help to:
Arthur McKenzie, Malcolm Dix, Peter Ratcliffe and Robin Varley.

A special thank-you to:
Ken Stobbs who stuck with me even when I threatened to become a boring zealot... and to the late Herb Sutherland who offered me so much help and encouragement.

1

It was an age in which too much of the world was changing too quickly. The giant trains that once inspired fear and awe as they belched out their smokestacks above the fields of Northumberland now only excited the children who had been told the Bogey Man would get them if they went too near the rail track.

People who had lived within ten miles of their birthplace all their lives were beginning to travel. Five men from Edith Lawson's village had returned from trips to Newcastle with tales of a huge city and great buildings and streets. Another villager, one of the drinking Robson family, even boasted that he had travelled to Scotland, though he later admitted that he had in fact fallen asleep on the train during his monthly trip to Alnwick market.

Recently Edith had been told of other inventions. Aeroplanes had taken to the skies and nearer home automobiles had begun to appear on the streets of Alnwick and Morpeth.

Edith had no idea where it would all lead. Then one day she saw the giant bailing machines appear in the fields of Milford at harvest time and she knew that the days of the horsemen were near their end. She knew that the world was getting smaller and more intrusive.

She told no one of her thoughts. Nor did she speak outside her family of her visits to the ancient stones that lay on the river bed about a mile west of Milford. There were some who said that these had once formed the mill from which the village had got its name. Others pointed out that a ford was an odd place to appoint a mill.

What could not be denied however was that this grotto had a magical, mystical quality in which the trees allowed the sun to twinkle through their boughs but for the most part held sway creating a velvet, gentle light that lived in harmony with the pleasing trickle of the river. It was a place that was strangely enclosed, a place where Edith felt compelled to pray, and a place where she sensed a communion of spirits, from the past.

Her holy place stood six miles down river from the village where she had been born and where she had met her husband, Jud.

As she looked up to the trees and saw the sunlight flitting through the leaves she recalled with Pavlovian certainty the first time she had seen him as he walked into her general dealer's store at Swannell. The sun shone directly on the shop front in the afternoons and he had stood framed in the doorway for some little time with the light so bright behind him, burning a halo on his unruly straw-coloured hair. He was very large and had a deep warm voice. His face, which she saw only after he advanced into the shop, was broad and cheerful. His blue eyes twinkled nicely, though set against perfection she thought them a trifle weak. She served him each summer after that and it got to be that come the first week in July each time the doorbell hopped and tinkled she would look up expectantly until the huge shadowy figure stood before her. He became a sign of the harvest and one year she met him while walking the lanes. She could smell the beer on him but his voice was soothing and rich and he didn't slur his words.

Free from the formal trappings of the shop she studied his face closer. He was a fine, handsome man; there was no denying it, a man who would always be followed by woman's glances. He told her his father had a sheep holding to the north west of Alnwick. Jud had extended his skills and every year he helped to tend the lambing and then hired himself out to the larger farms.

He was proud of his work. He could stack the hay so straight that it could withstand the strongest wind, and he could tell when a stack needed funnelling against fire by merely pushing his fist into the hay and feeling the heat. He slept in the fields at night and in a barn if it was raining. To Edith his life seemed nomadic, exciting, and romantic.

The two of them got to talking and walking each summer and then in '94 he told her that "the grief" had taken his father.

"The grief?" She did not understand.

He explained that husbands and wives who lived in

remote regions became so strongly linked that they usually died within a year of each other. His father had lasted six years but now "the grief" had taken him and he was in decline.

Jud stared softly at Edith as he told her that this would be his last year in Swannell as he could no longer leave his father on his own all summer.

Edith felt numb. All she could think of was that her own parents had died within a year of each other but had not been particularly close. In fact they'd disliked each other. However it didn't seem appropriate or even relevant to mention this at that moment.

There was a silence which spoke of their feelings more than they had ever spoken of them. He looked at her. Her brown hair was parted in the middle and swept to the back of her head where it was held in a bun. He wondered what she would look like with her hair hanging long and loose. Perhaps her high, straight carriage hid a more voluptuous nature. Perhaps the steady grey eyes would shine in passion. He wanted to know.

They stopped by a hedge and Jud picked one of the wild pink roses. He offered it to her and she took it gently. "I don't suppose you'd like to get married girl?" His voice shook with shyness.

She merely smiled in answer. She thought it touching that such a big man could be so hesitant. She had tired of Swannell. She knew the lives of the villagers so well that she could see her own future among them.

They walked further that evening and made love in a little wood to the north of the village; it was as though they'd made a bond to their agreement. They married at Swannell church that August. She sold her shop a week before the wedding and they moved north to live with Jud's father while they looked for a cottage of their own.

Mr Lawson, as she called him, was tall, thin, and stooped with age. He welcomed them: "Best come in." He was not a talkative man, indeed there were days when he hardly spoke at all save to occasionally call out his dead wife's name as he stared with watery eyes into the kitchen fire. He noticed little, not even that Edith was with child, though he made it plain he expected her to do the house chores.

One morning , shortly after the turn of the year, they

found him dead in his old wooden chair. Apparently he had risen in the night for one last conversation with his wife.

Edith was relieved at his passing. Her first son, Harold, was born three months later.

She took to life on the hill farm better than she had expected. Ironically it was Jud who could not settle in his own home. He said his father's ghost appeared in every chair and he found it hard to lay him to rest.

He began to look for a new farm and when one of the travelling tinkers told him of land for sale at Milford he acted with rare decision and speed.

The holding lay in a thin strip along the southern ridge of the valley and the slope was such that Farmer Norton could not risk his machines on it. He was forced to graze cattle and when a couple of them broke legs slipping on the steep slope after heavy rain he decided to make the best of a bad job and sell up. Jud walked the dozen miles to Alnwick on the Saturday after he'd heard of the sale. He took the train to Swannell and walked the five miles to the farm. By the time he met up with Mr Norton his shirt was clinging like a second skin under his jacket and his flat cap was making his hair itch. His tanned skin had turned red and his blond hair was damp. He was tired but he talked excitedly as he walked along the valley. The men made an odd contrast for Farmer Norton was small and dapper. Not like a farmer to the casual eye. His bowler hat and shoulder cloak would not have been given a second glance in the town but Jud knew he was a man of the land after they had spoken a couple of sentences.

At last they climbed the ridge. "Well there she is." Mr Norton had taken off his bowler and was drumming the inside with his fingers. "There she is."

Jud looked at the stone cottage, part sheltered from the west wind by a cluster of elms and ash trees. He felt the land and knew it was good. A gust of wind lifted Mr Norton's shoulder cloak and then was gone. The sky was full of clouds but they were high, white, and still. Jud could feel the sudden stillness of it all. He felt as though he was standing in a moment in time and was intoxicated.

"I'll take it," he said.

Mr Norton laughed and combed his fingers through his thick, grey hair. "You don't want to see inside?"

"Well, yes." Jud was anxious not to appear a fool.

The cottage was dry and smelt of newly baked bread. The walls were whitewashed. There were two rooms upstairs and three down including a small kitchen and a converted byre.

"We used to be able to reach out and touch the family cow." Mr Norton gave a dry laugh. "Warmed us in the winter night."

"I'll take it," said Jud, not listening.

"Hold on man. You can't do business like that."

"Why not?"

"Well..." Mr Norton hesitated. His fingers combed his hair again. "Well there are agents to see and papers to sign."

"Oh," said Jud. "Well I'll still take it and here's my hand on the matter."

The farmer hesitated before taking Jud's hand. "Alright. Have it your own way. It's a deal then."

They spat on their hands and shook to seal the bargain.

"I've got land to sell," said Jud.

Farmer Norton shrugged. "I've got matters to tie up here. I'll give you up to six months before looking for another sale."

Jud nodded. "That's fair."

It took Jud five months to sell his farm and by the time the strain of dealing with lawyers and agents and other such foreign things were lifted from him Edith was pregnant again. They hired a tall-backed cart and broke the journey with an overnight stay at Swannell. The cart bulged with their belongings." Jud smiled at the sight. "Reminds you of flitting day," he said.

"My God," Edith was struck by a thought. "It's Harold's birthday." They looked at the tiny figure asleep in a wooden cot that was stuck between them and burst into laughter.

"He'll never forgive us if he ever finds out." Edith started to giggle a light falsetto against Jud's deep rich laugh.

She glanced across at him as he steered the cart. His eyes were set on the road and he had begun to hum softly. It was one of the most enjoyable days of his life. Everything that was behind him was behind him and the future lay clear and simple which was how he liked it.

Their home stood on the ridge of the river valley, about a mile from the main street of Milford. The farmhouse was seventy or eighty feet up from the river level but partly hidden behind a cluster of trees. They could hear the church bell though on a Sunday morning and from his new home Jud could look out and see the patchwork history of the fields. This was what he knew. The summer would come and there would be the gold of the wheat, the grey yellow of the barley, the sprinkled green of the sugar beets, the light green of the fodder maize and the richness of the pasture land. He knew it with the certainty that he had come to accept and know nature and he could not wait to meet the challenge of it once more on this, his new land.

The village had once owed its existence to the flour mill in days when the river had run swifter, but now it stayed alive through the pitmen. The original mine to the south of Milford had long since ceased to yield coal and the broken pit wheel remained, still and rotting. The colliers now worked a new seam, two miles to the north east. At six o'clock each morning they slipped from their cottages, flat-capped, thick booted, and cupping their hands to their mouths to blow warmth into their fingers. They jogged from the village with their bait tins slapping against their thighs, their calls and laughter rising ragged in the crisp early air. Jud came to know them and accept them, to the point where he viewed some of them as friends.

Daniel was born four months after they moved into their new home. He came on the hottest afternoon of the summer of ninety six. Edith had moved into Harold's room at the front of the house to escape the worst of the sun. She lay there panting and weak after her labour, glad of the cool, thick, stone walls, and the draught that Jud had created by opening all doors and windows.

Mrs McGrath, a miner's wife, who acted as the village midwife, waddled up and downstairs calling continually: "Everything's alright, pet. Everything's perfect."

They were alone with the baby. Jud who wouldn't show fear to a bull had edged his cap round in his hands and said. "Well pet I'll just take the wee 'un out of the way eh."

Edith smiled at the memory. He was just the same when he wanted to go out to the pub. She was stronger than him. Her strength had helped her endure her pain and now it was all over she allowed her eyes to close and lay contented as though in a dream.

Mrs McGrath came to her holding the baby in a white flannel towel that stood out against her long brown dress. The women who had scarce met an hour before the birth felt a bond from the experience.

Mrs McGrath looked down at Edith's face that was smooth in peace. "Are you awake Missus?" She whispered loudly. Edith allowed her lids to lift and her eyes rested on the baby. He had the blond hair of his father.

Mrs McGrath smiled. "I've been bringing babbies into the world for thirty year or more and this is the bonniest of the lot of them and that's a fact." She leaned the baby forward to give the mother a better look. The boy gave a little belch and his eyes closed in sleep.

Mrs McGrath rocked the baby humming softly. She looked down at Edith. She too was asleep. The midwife laid the baby in a wooden cot and moved it gently to the side of the bed.

"I suppose I'd best be making tea for her man," she murmured to herself. She remembered how he had fled the house with the boy. She looked from the upstairs window along the field. There was no sign of the two of them. "Likely he'll be stopping out till he's sure it's all over," she told herself.

She went downstairs to the kitchen and stood enjoying the stillness. The house felt empty. There was a strong sense of peace about it. She could hear the silence and it was beautiful and in that moment life was beautiful.

Much later, Edith woke to the pleasing sound of an axe on wood. She looked across to the cot and smiled. "We'll call him Daniel," she decided suddenly.

2

Jud's land had lain fallow the previous year and Farmer Norton had agreed to sow wheat in his two largest fields so that the crop would lay ready the summer that Jud moved in.

Jud worked hard in the sun, pleased to possess the land as a child would a toy.

He walked the boundary enjoying his ownership in a physical sense. This was his, he told himself, and he was pleased by the emotion which echoed the thought.

There were many who chuckled when word got out that Jud intended to scythe the field right along the ridge. On all the surrounding holdings, the scythe was used merely to cut the first lane for the harvesting machine.

Jud had a stranger's sensitivity to such interest and for weeks as the wheat ripened he became increasingly irritable.

One evening when Jud snapped at Harold for dropping some of his supper on the floor Edith took the boy's side.

"He's but a baby Jud. It's you who's in the wrong not he." She left the table upset. Jud gave a sniff, picked up his tools and began to clean and sharpen them on the front porch. He shouted through the door: "God help us woman, can you not realise the worry I have at present?"

"Aye," Edith retorted immediately. "And more than you can realise the worry in others." She always argued like that and always won. She was sharper than Jud and more cutting. Jud muttered something to himself and began to polish furiously at the scythe.

He was up first the following morning. He picked up his bait tin and was gone before Edith came down.

This annoyed her as he knew it would. She felt duty bound to make him breakfast when he had a long day at work.

"Well let him act the child," she muttered to herself, but

the words did little to sooth her irritation and her guilt.

Jud had cut half of a lane down the far side of the smallest field when he became aware that he was being watched. He looked round and saw Old Willum leaning against his stick at a low point in the boundary hedge.

The two men had hardly spoken but he knew Old Willum to be held in esteem by miners and farmers alike. He had fought in the Crimean War and it was rumoured that he had taken part in a great charge on the Russian guns. He never spoke of it, though he would talk for hours of the old days in the village and of other country matters.

Jud had gone as far as to ask Jack Robson the postman why Willum was called "Old" for he looked to be merely in his sixties. The postie had nodded his head slowly as he imparted an important bit of village folklore. He leaned towards Jud as though imparting a great secret, There was, he said, a history of growing old in the family. Consequently Willum's father had been known as Old Tom and his grandfather as Old David, so Willum had been called Old Willum from childhood.

Old Willum was facing the sun staring straight at Jud. He had pulled his cap forward so his eyes were in the shade but Jud knew the old man was watching his every move. He became filled with self consciousness and almost at once his work became ragged. The long sweeps of his scythe lost their rhythm and the more that irritated him the worse his work became. He was a fool to go on and he knew it, but the knowledge only drove him on. The sweat began to stream down his body and his hair and moustache were soon dank. He looked back at the uneven stubble in the field and could stand it no more.

"Have you not got anything better to do," he shouted.

Old Willum was startled by his aggressive tone. "Are you annoyed at something?" He sucked on a long blade of grass.

"I don't like being laughed at." Jud said shortly, already conscious that he was being absurd.

"I aint laughing Jud."

Jud stared at Old Willum who was leaning on his stick not the least perturbed by the confrontation.

"I thought you were laughing at my scything," Jud said sullenly.

"No." Old Willum gestured to the whippet at his feet. "I've come to catch a couple of rabbits and have a day in the sun."

The anger left Jud as suddenly as it had come. He glanced across to the mass of uncut wheat. "I reckon it'll be a few hours before you're in business," he said.

Old Willum stood as still as history. "I can wait."

Jud shrugged and went back to his work. He was feeling more at one with himself now. In another hour he had worked his way round to the old man again and by this time he felt it time to take a bite of food. He offered the old man a cheese and onion sandwich but Willum shook his head. "Always gives my stomach a rest on Mondays."

Jud nodded in understanding, "Except for beer eh."

Old Willum smiled showing his stained brown teeth.

Jud took a further two hours to do three more laps and at the end of it he surveyed the virgin patch in the centre of the field.

It stood about sixty yards by twenty five, swaying shyly in the breeze. The scent of the fallen wheat hung heavy in the air.

"Reckon that's about right." Jud hitched up a stretch of his trousers that had slipped below his broad leather belt.

Old Willum nodded and leaned forward in expectation as Jud walked slowly to the far side of the patch.

"Is the dog ready?" he shouted. The whippet was yapping away by now. "Right then." Jud began to scythe his way through the middle of the patch shouting wildly as he went. He hadn't gone five yards before a terrified rabbit squirted from the far side and the dog gave a yelp of excitement.

The rabbit squealed as it zig zagged from the whippets snapping teeth. Jud and Willum were intoxicated by the chase and they shouted encouragement each time the dog seemed to close with its prey. The rabbit tried to make for the sanctuary of the hedge but each time it looked like escaping the dog was there to cut it off. At last the whippet's teeth caught one of the rabbit's rear legs and death was certain. Old Willum gripped his cap tightly as the dog closed with the frantic animal. The rabbit's last cry was heard two fields away. When the whippet brought it back its neck was snapped.

That evening Jud whistled as he brought two rabbits

home. He was honest enough to remember his surliness with Harold and played with him on the floor as he waited for his tea. When he was happy Jud demanded that others shared the feeling and that night his fingers scurried playfully over Edith's waist as she stood with her back to him at the sink. She wriggled and laughed and scolded him.

"Behave Jud Lawson or you'll have me dropping the plates." But all the while she was enjoying the warmth in him and they both knew that she was pleased. The worry was lifted from their home and the rooms rang with laughter.

Usually Jud could not sit still in the evenings and he whistled furiously as he busied himself with some task.

For the first three years he was too busy to think of anything but the farm during the day and in the evening he would make a chair or a table, clean his tools, or work on repairs to the cottage.

He took his children out like toys, playing with them for a while until he lost interest. The trouble was he couldn't put them back in a box for by then the boys would be charged with excitement and he couldn't put them down.

Finally he would say: "Now look you enough is enough. I've things to do. "But Harold and Daniel would only laugh until he was forced to shout back at them or make some excuse and leave to do some work as Edith tutted.

"You're like a leaf in the wind. You've the mind of a butterfly Jud Lawson." she shook her head in disapproval.

"I've got work to do, woman." His face became sullen. But they both knew it was only half true.

He did not like Edith to confront him with his own inadequacies though he did nothing to overcome them. He sulked for a while and then escaped from the mood like a change in the weather, appearing once more as the good-humoured, warm-hearted, but essentially aimless man that he was.

Edith would catch Harold staring sadly at his father. He seemed to see right into their rows. He had a perception which was uncanny and his young face was always serious as he demanded facts and information. His brow frowned when he asked a question, and that, and his slightly wayward fair hair gave him a look older then his years. She loved him. She saw in him a steadiness and determination which were lacking in Jud. She caressed his hair, trying to straighten the parting.

Edith accepted life's rhythm better than Jud. Her belief in God was strong and unthinking. She could have lived in a hundred worlds and fitted into every one, as long as they did not threaten her sons. She spent most of her evenings knitting, sewing, or baking bread or thick scones in the large oven built into the chimney by the kitchen fire.

In the winter the boys were allowed to undress in front of the burning coal and lie looking at the flames as Edith worked.

Harold peppered her with questions. He wanted to know everything. "Why are balls round? What is air? How does the sun come up? Where does the moon come from?" And all the while he frowned with impatience. Daniel's face was broader and his eyes were wide and large He hardly spoke unless a question was directed at him. He seemed content to stare dreaming into the flames.

The church bell called to them each Sunday and Edith hurried and fussed before she took the boys into the village. She lived in fear of arriving late and walking down the aisle with every eye on her. It had happened twice because of Jud's tardiness. His amiability left him insensitive to such things. Nowadays she did not press him when he excused himself from churchgoing on the grounds of work.

As the boys grew older Jud took Harold and later Daniel for walks on Sunday afternoons.

Jud looked forward to them as much as the boys. Not only did he enjoy the scenery but he used the walks to absolve himself of Edith's accusations of his lack of interest in his sons. Often, in the summer, they rambled up the river until it was little more than a sprinkling stream. All three of them liked best to take the road into the hills. They walked until the clouds lay at the end of each twist in the road. Daniel would shout excitedly: "Look Dad. We're walking into heaven." Harold and Jud laughed every time and Daniel beamed with pleasure.

They preferred autumn when the air was crisp and the russet leaves were clinging to the trees. On perfect days the dusk was just beginning to chill the boys as they arrived home and in the darkened kitchen the flames danced from the grill as their mother made girdle cakes which she served with melting butter.

The cakes were the grand finale to the great day and even Jud watched the boys in amusement as he rocked his chair by the fire.

Harold and Daniel began to play with the colliers' sons in the village. They tried to ape their elders by challenging each other to games of pitch and toss at the back of the King George until the men chased them away. In the summer they roamed in packs along the river bank and in the wood higher up. They tried to build a stockade to play Mafeking but after a day or two Harold lost interest in the game, declaring it rather childish. Daniel stared in disbelief. He found it so exciting in the woods; it was a world of its own.

The summers passed all too quickly and the boys were sent to the village school in Swannell. They walked the five miles each morning and back in the afternoon without a care. Harold and Daniel had their father's immunity to the weather but some of the colliers' sons hated the rain and wind. Larry Collins was the worst of them and he spent much of the journey complaining about the cold. Everyone accepted that Larry was the tough boy of the village so Daniel was startled to find him so vulnerable

3

Jud used drink to escape from boredom. In the early days he would visit the pub every Friday and Saturday but as time passed he increased the frequency of his visits until he was drinking every night.

Edith despised him for it and for the way he wriggled with excuses. For at least ten minutes before he left his home he would walk up and down, or fidget in his pockets, or laugh loudly at the least witty thing said.

Sometimes he would announce: "Well then, I'm off for a walk," and would give a weak grin. Other nights Edith, with a mixture of kindness and cruelty, said in a cold voice: "For heavens sake Jud, stop going on as though you're walking on a pin cushion and get yourself out. We all know where you're going."

There was no indignity, no contempt that could stop him. Once free from the cottage he felt released like a prisoner leaving jail. Inside his home he was a restless man with nowhere to go. On the walk to the King George however he was content, whistling all the way and nodding cheerfully to anyone he met.

The King George stood on a rise in the road that ran along by the river, which was just as well because every couple of years or so the water would swell over the banks flooding the gardens of the neighbouring cottages. Each time it happened Len Harkin, the owner of the inn grinned and told his customers: "My God man! But for good fortune my barrels would be bobbing like barges in my cellar. Look at those poor blighters across the road."

Then one year he stopped after someone pointed out that "those poor blighters across the road" were in fact his customers.

Once in the King George Jud leaned hugely against the bar, half listening to the voices and laughter that cut through the smoky air.

For the first three pints of heavy, dark beer he rarely spoke more than courtesy demanded. Then after the first hour or so his sense of being a spectator would wane and he would plunge into all the arguments. The miners formed the hard core of the George's customers. Some of them called on their way from work and left after a couple of pints; some stayed late and others came after they'd had an evening meal.

They were full of their union and their rights and Jud loved to bait them; to tell them that he was a self-made man, and that they could do what he had done, if they had the will. He told them these half truths until the miners shouted him down and a huge grin would light up his face. He was always friendly with them, but even so he enjoyed believing he was superior.

Of all the miners who came to the King George there was only one, Willie Collins, who could match Jud for size and strength.

Willie's hair, like his son Larry's, was black as the coal he dug. He was a man who had to be coaxed. He had none of Jud's openness and in drink his dark eyes frowned and the word soon passed around that Big Billy was brooding and men stayed their distance. Only Jud did not fear him. Drink filled his senses giving him a feeling of belief and certainty. This made him happy and generous and it never crossed his mind that others might not be the same as he.

It was in this spirit that he agreed to arm wrestle with Billy one Friday night. Everyone was carried away with the drink and they started to lay bets against one man or the other quicker than at a whippet race. Only Len Harkin shifted uneasily from one foot to the other, but he knew it was too late to stop the contest and his eyes glanced for reassurance under the bar to the long axe handle that his father had placed there before him.

Jud and Willie faced each other over a cleared table. A few drops of beer were spilled at each end of the wooden surface and the first man to wet the other's hand was to be judged the winner.

Johnny McGuire, the husband of the village midwife, started the contest by clapping his hands, and then they were at it elbow to elbow. Willie began to redden with effort and a slow smile spread across Jud's face, his "stupid grin", as Edith called it. Both their bodies leaned forward with intense effort, yet for seconds their arms stayed strangely still and then their hands began to quiver as their arms bulged with the strain. They continued like this for minutes until Jud began to prevail. It was probably his innocence that gave him the vital strength for while he never gave a thought to losing as the minutes went by Willie became aware that, for the first time in his life, he had met a man who was at least his equal and this disturbed him until his resolution became tempered with anger, desperation, and finally panic. It was thus that he lost concentration for a vital second and in that second Jud forced his hand off centre, and from there on there was no going back.

Willie's red face twisted with a strange mixture of anger and frustration as slowly, but inexorably, his hand was pushed down further and further until it hovered right over the spilled beer. The miners were roaring both men on and even Len Harkin forgot his apprehension and he shouted along with the rest of them as Willie's hand was finally spread on the table.

There were some among the crowd who half hoped for trouble for they reckoned that the big farmer would be more than a match for Willie who'd scattered the teeth of more than one of them at the back of the George. But both men were too exhausted to talk and they slumped over the table like a couple of drunks. By the time they had recovered Len Harkin had presented them with a pint each and Jud was saying generously that arm wrestling was only a knack.

"The only man who's beaten me was a little un. But he had the knack." He grinned. "He taught me how to do it. Now if Willie here had the knack there'd not be a man in England as could stand against him."

When he was happy he scattered compliments like seed at sowing time, and though he did it purely because he was happy, and without motive or purpose, it still won him respect.

It was a good night for Jud. He could feel the beer intoxicating him, shortening his vision, until all he could see was that which pleased him.

He started to sing in his deep voice and others joined in until the sound of their songs bellowed out across the village, almost as far as the church bell on a Sunday. Some of the kiddies heard the noise as they lay in their beds and they cuddled into each other hoping that when their dads got home they wouldn't shout at their mums.

Jud sang on until the sound of his voice filled him with exhilaration. He ended with a solo rendition of Bless This House, bowed to the applause and bid the company goodnight.

Neither the wind nor the rain bothered him on the way home, even though he had no coat. Once out of the light of the village his progress became slower. The moon was near full but it was hidden for most of the way home by the rain clouds and Jud had to rely on his memory of the path for most of the way. At last he could see the light from the cottage and it drew him like a moth to flame. He knew that Edith would be waiting for him. She always did since the night he'd fallen asleep at the door.

His jacket was soaked through and the rain had made ringlets of his hair, flooding his eyebrows so that he had difficulty in seeing.

Edith looked at him as he closed the door and noticed a slight sway in his huge frame.

"You fool," she said coldly. "Look at you. You utter fool."

Jud's face closed sulkily. Edith had a rough towel warming in the hearth and she flung it at him contemptuously. ""Here. Get yourself dried. If you are able."

"I'm not a bloody child." Jud's voice could not disguise his hurt.

"Oh no! Well you certainly behave like one." Jud had the strength to snap her in two but she had the tongue to whip him to pieces. She had self discipline and self control. Jud had an affinity with the seasons. He was disciplined by Nature but other than that discipline was not natural to him. He glowered at her then slung his shirt over his head after a pause that was sufficiently long to persuade himself that he was not doing her bidding.

"Now don't start on me tonight cos I've had enough see." He glowered as his head emerged from the soaking shirt.

"More than enough I'd say." She could smell the beer across the room.

Jud was breathing heavily. His nostrils flared. He leaned forward on the kitchen table trying to intimidate her. "Now just don't start. I'm warning you." He lifted his hands to give emphasis to the words and Edith seized the moment.

"Strike me and it'll be the last blow you'll ever strike."

Jud stared stupidly at her, confused by this new attack.

"Your supper's getting cold." She dismissed him.

She knew he hated it when she treated him like this, scolding him as though he were a child. She knew it and delighted in it. She saw it as her way of punishing him. Usually she bared his sense of guilt and forced him shamefacedly to bed but this time he had drunk too much to show such sensitivity.

He smashed his fist down on to the table making his pie and potatoes leap. "You call this food for a man!" he shouted.

"Aye I do. More than enough for the likes of you," she cried.

And with that they were at it. He bellowing like a bull and she, quicker, snapping at his heels like a terrier, until the two of them were only stopped by the sight of Harold standing in the half light at the door with his shirt tails flapping in the draught.

"I can't sleep," he sobbed.

Here again Edith was quicker than her husband. "Come here me darling," she cried holding out her hand and clasping the boy to her. "It's alright there's nothing to worry about." She kissed him and pulled his head into her breast. "See what you've done," she said as she walked to the stairs leaving Jud standing like a stranger in his own home.

Jud lowered his head into his hands and allowed his fingers to furrow through his hair. He suddenly felt very tired. It should have been a great night after his victory at the George. But it wasn't.

The incident filled them both with guilt but neither spoke of it. Secretly Edith was happy enough to see Jud out of the way. She was content at nights with her knitting or sewing or reading. It was the thought that he was avoiding his responsibilities rather than his absence that annoyed her. They only came together now over trivial things. Edith laid out sticks and coal each night in preparation for the morning. She would warm a bowl of water in the oven above the fire for Jud but he rarely used it. Even in the worst of the winter he plunged his arms into a sink of freezing water and scooped it over his head. He always grinned hugely as she looked on. Whenever Edith watched this little scene she wondered how a man so weak could be so tough. The sight of her watching him as she sat shoulders over elbows amused him.

"Aye but you're lucky to have a fine chap like me." He grinned as he stood straight and handsome.

"Some feel the cold more than others." There were times when she was reluctant to give him the space to breathe.

At other times however she would allow his good humour to infect her, and encouraged, he would pursue her round the kitchen reaching for her with his big fingers.

Either that or he would take a stand in front of the big mirror and say: "Mind missus I don't know how you landed a fine chap like me." Then she would snap and scold him. "Get away with you, you big daft man; preening yourself in front of a mirror like some lass."

"Like a lass is it," he roared full of laughter. "A funny lass, missus, and that's a fact."

These were the times that they were closest now and the children seized on them like starving mites at a banquet, laughing and roaring to match Jud's guffaws.

When he had left for work and the children had marched off to school Edith used the mirror herself. She glided in front of it with false casualness and stood staring in regret.

She had a proud, upright stance; her back was as straight as a stick, but her face was showing signs of age and tiredness now. The brown hair was streaked with white running from her forehead. She had wide, grey eyes and a strong nose and chin but her skin was dry and her neck and body were thickening.

One day the mirror annoyed her so much, drawing her to it, making her see things that she didn't want to see, that she had used it to irritate Jud, knowing the pleasure he took in it.

"It's a dreadful thing, Jud, a cumbersome, ugly thing. Let's take it down." She glanced at him quickly.

"Thou daresn't touch that missus. Any road, it's too big for anyone but me to shift." He paused before advancing with a new argument. "Besides it lifts the room with its light and without it it'd be too dark half the time for Harold to do his studying."

The years rolled on as the routine of their life blended one day into another. Then, suddenly, a big event made Edith realize that time was moving on.

4

Harold was the first boy from the village to win a scholarship to the town school in Alnwick and Edith never tired of the fact.

She remembered the ache of boredom of her childhood days in Swannell, she saw her inevitable future in Milford, so Harold's new horizons became her own and they excited her.

She took him to school on the first day. It was as much her day as Harold's and she scolded Jud whenever he tried to take part.

She was up first. Jud followed her downstairs and this irritated her. They were all seated before breakfast was ready and Daniel stared silently at Harold who shone in his maroon blazer with grey edging.

Jud patted him on the shoulder. "Now don't you let yourself be bullied by those town kids."

Edith rapped her knife down on the thick wooden table. "What kind of advice is that?" She snapped. "He's going to school to learn, not to fight."

"I know boys and I know school," Jud retorted defensively.

"Your school. You couldn't fall down in your school. This," she paused grandly, "is a big school. Why, some of the boys even come to class in cars or carriages."

"Go, not come mother," said Harold, anxious to intervene in her verbal whipping before it became so complete that it set the mood for the day.

He broke up the conversation by walking to Jud's huge mirror where he stood straightening his maroon tie. They all watched in silence as he twisted this way and that checking his appearance until Daniel started to laugh.

Straight after breakfast Edith took Harold to the front door with such suddenness that he had to break away to wish his father and brother goodbye. Jud smiled and ran his fingers through Harold's hair. "I'm so sorry," he said in a correct tone that mocked Edith. "You'll just have to comb it again now."

Edith was so full of herself and the great day that she could not see the joke. "Come on Harold," she said stiffly. "I'll just have to do it on the train." Harold. Jud and Daniel were laughing at her prissiness by now. Harold was relieved that the snap had gone out of the atmosphere.

Edith was dressed in her best coat. It was the colour of dark chocolate and she had stuck a violet in her lapel.

She wore no hat, she never did, but instead of putting her hair in the normal plain bun she had parted it in the middle, sending two waves looping down on either side of her forehead to be gathered at the back by a brown ribbon tied in a neat bow.

She chattered gaily on the way to the station, pointing out every bird, every flower, that caught her eye. Harold thought that the most impressive thing about her knowledge was that she was unaware of it.

She was in the same state of excitement for the thirty minutes it took the train to reach Alnwick. It was a perfect day for early autumn. The leaves were burnished by the low sun and the air was crisp and clean. Even the bustle in the town could not distract from the sense of nature in the air. Edith chattered her way down the hill, past Bondgate and the awesome castle, pulling a collar straight here and spotting a loose thread there.

Harold became increasingly agitated. He wanted to escape into the peace of his own thoughts. He clasped his mother's hand and said: "Don't worry I'll be alright. Really."

"Yes of course you will," she said, not understanding and Harold had to wait until the sight of the school stilled her.

The Royal school was a long, flat-faced, two-storey building with ten chimney stacks spaced at regular intervals along the roof. The facade stretched for at least eighty yards forming a background to the huge-tree lined playing field that lay before it. A row of firs stood like sentries along the red-brick front wall that had an arched gate at its centre.

Harold smiled and Edith leapt in. "What?" she demanded. "What is so amusing?"

Harold gestured to the firs. "If Daniel was here he'd be

telling us that they were soft wood and then he'd give us a lecture about the advantages of deciduous trees or some such thing."

Edith contented herself with a little tutt.

A stone path ran parallel to the walls, under the lining of trees. Edith's eye followed it to the high arched school entrance. She was by now utterly in awe. She had never seen anything so grand in her life. Not even the squire's mansion at Alverston could compare with this. Groups of pupils were standing in front of the school and a lad of about seventeen with dark hair and a shiny face approached them. "Can I help you, madam?" He smiled while assessing them.

Harold blushed. He was glad his mother had dressed in her best coat. He was so overwhelmed by the school that for a few seconds he assumed that everything about the place was right and that everything his mother did that seemed foreign to it must be wrong.

He washed away such thoughts in a wave of guilt. Even so, though he had never doubted his brain against anyone, as he looked at this self-assured youth he became acutely aware that the boy possessed a sense of style that he had not known had even existed until this morning.

He emerged from these thoughts to find that his mother had asked the youth a question which he had answered and his mother was smiling and bobbing a curtsy. He saw the glint of amusement in the lad's face and suddenly felt vulnerable.

"Mother," he whispered as they walked through the main entrance. "Please get off the stage.

"Don't be silly Harold," she smiled at the other boy. "This is what's known as a mannered society."

Harold felt his soul curdle. He was a sensitive boy at a sensitive time, desperately trying to erect his own defences to life so that he could go on the attack.

His mother was gaining in self confidence by the minute. She knocked on the headmaster's door as though he owed her money. Harold felt another stab of panic as the great man summoned them in. It took an act of courage not to scuttle back down the corridor. Mr. Jenkins was sitting at his large mahogany desk. Behind him the sun was warming the stained glass window, rippling the room with colours.

As Mr. Jenkins rose from his desk with a smile Harold felt the breath of life pass through him once more.

His eyes bored into Harold demanding attention. He glanced down at the papers he was holding in his left hand. "Ah yes, Lawson, the scholarship boy." He had a deep voice. He was, Harold guessed, in his late fifties. His grey hair grew as fierce as a thicket and wisps of it sprung from his large ears and hung like spider plants.

"Yes," Edith nodded and smiled.

Mr. Jenkins didn't seem to pause, but said with the effortless authority of a headmaster in his own school: "Please Mrs. Lawson allow the lad to answer for himself." He spoke the words quietly and Harold noted that he had used the word lad instead of boy. Lad sounded friendlier and he began to feel if not a rapport, at least an interest, in what the great man was saying. They began to discuss his work, his knowledge and his progress. Harold could feel his mother's silence. She sat like a stranger amid this foreign talk. The rest of the interview passed affably as Harold gained in confidence.

At last it was finished and Mr. Jenkins told Edith that Harold would be assigned to form 3a that term with the prospect of promotion at Christmas if he did well enough.

"Though I'm sure that's a foregone conclusion if you work hard enough." Mr. Jenkins smiled. "The engine's there, Mrs. Lawson. The engine's there. It's up to us to provide the fuel." He smiled and patted Harold on the head.

Harold felt forged by the experience as he escorted his mother back to the school entrance. They stopped at the gate and she began to take charge once more.

"Now don't let them overawe you." She stroked a wayward hair on her son's head.

Harold shook his head firmly. "Do stop it mother. I'm not a child."

Edith laughed. "Of course you're not but..." she searched for the correct word and failed so she said. "Oh I'm off to town. I'll see you at four."

She was as good as her word and that afternoon when Harold approached the stone, arched gate she was standing across the street viewing the school with the eye of a part owner.

She watched as first a bobble of boys and then a stream

of them clattered down the path. She saw Harold straight away. His new uniform stood out like a new penny. She beamed with pride. How smart he looked with his maroon blazer and cap. He was walking slowly with a group of boys chatting animatedly. Before he spoke she knew he had lost his nervousness and that he was at home with these lads and for a brief, crazy moment she felt that she was an outsider.

For the second or third time that day she was relieved to be in her finest clothes. As soon as he saw her he broke away from his friends and waved as he trotted across the empty road. She did not want to meet any of the boys because she was sure that Harold could impress them more than she could and that was what mattered.

Edith took her son by the hand pressing it with affection as they walked towards the station.

Harold did not wait for her questions and began to talk with bubbling excitement about the day.

She couldn't keep up with his torrent of observations. "Good heavens Harold. Slow down," she said laughing with the pleasure of it. "There'll be nothing left to tell when you get home and I'll have to listen to it all again." She hugged him. Harold grinned. They were both high with the excitement of the day and closer to each other than at any other time. The journey home was full of anticipation. There would be so much to tell the others. Edith escorted him from the station as though he were a prince. She stopped everyone on the way home to tell them about her son. All the while, as Edith threw out small talk like rice at a wedding, Harold stood silent and ill at ease in his uniform. He knew there would be some who would scorn him for it. He shifted from one leg to the other beginning to resent his mother. It seemed that he existed for her vanity, and he was getting hungry.

"Mayn't I go mother I'm starving?"

Edith turned, her eyes wide with surprise. "Why surely Harold. I'll catch you in a minute."

Harold knew she would follow him because she would not want to miss his homecoming and the cascade of news and questions that went with it.

He had hardly gone twenty yards before she made an excuse about getting the lad's meal ready (though it had

27

been roasting in the fire oven all day) and he heard the clatter of her feet as she scurried after him.

Jud and Daniel were waiting for him. Jud had left the repair work on his long fence so that he would be home when his son arrived and he plied the boy with questions.

There was no day so sweet at the Royal as the first. Despite the irritations of his mother's behaviour Harold had recognised the bond between them when faced with something that mutually excited them.

Time passed and the family settled into a routine. Harold had to catch the train each morning from Swannell about half an hour before the village lads were due at school. Daniel walked the road with him each morning, relieved that the time difference did not allow the other boy's to see Harold in his uniform.

Harold had become an outsider to the other boys but he was protected from their scorn by the natural detachment that his desire to study afforded him. He did not play their games any longer; he seldom roamed the river bank or joined the primitive packs of boys as they played in the woods.

He was proud of his achievements in the same way that Jud was proud of his farming.

The uniform, the studying, which he enjoyed, gave his life a meaning, a purpose. He could see himself in the future, see that he had a future, and that pleased him.

Daniel felt a terrible pull between the village boys and his brother. He was a boy who loved to play games. He lived in the excitement of them and he escaped into them with total involvement. He read a great deal too, mainly the wild adventure stories that Harold dismissed with lofty words. He did have one ability over his brother however, the ability to read at great speed. Harold noticed it one afternoon as he watched Daniel's eyes dart from line to line. He assumed that Daniel was just flitting through the book until one weekend he found Daniel reading a Walter Scott novel which Harold had brought back from the Royal. He questioned his brother about the plot and the characters and was given an assured answer in every instance.

Daniel's abilities were also noticed by the village schoolmaster, Mr. Jessup, who had coached Harold to such good effect.

Mr. Jessup was a small, mild-mannered man with a

small-featured face and bright blue eyes that peered out on the world from behind an ancient pair of rimless spectacles. He was a man whom people passed in the street without noticing, but as a teacher he was a rarity in his time...he wanted every boy who passed through his classes to advance himself in some way.

He had hoped at first that Daniel would go on to the Royal like his brother. Certainly he had the ability. But he discovered as the terms went by that the boy did not have the same ambition. Also he had a private self which he would not reveal.

Mr. Jessup often discussed his pupils with his wife Emily, a kindly woman who looked out for all the children. She had taken a special interest in Daniel ever since she had come across "a rather beautiful child" while walking the lane one windy day. "He was standing in the middle of the road staring up at a kestrel," she said.

Mr. Jessup looked up from his book of verse. "That would be Daniel," he said.

Emily chuckled at the memory. "He told me that kestrels hovered by flying into the wind at exactly the same speed as the wind."

Mr. Jessup smiled. "He is a very bright but idiosyncratic boy. He's the brother of Harold, the scholarship boy."

Emily picked up a cloth and lifted the iron kettle from the kitchen fire.

She began to pour the boiling water into a large, china teapot. "When he watched the bird it was as if he was living the moment with the kestrel. There was this strange affinity."

Mr. Jessup knew there was no retreat into his book. "He is the strangest boy I have ever taught." He paused as he tried to round up his thoughts to elaborate. "He does not seek information as his brother did. It's as though he wants to feel life as a musician feels music." He sighed. "I don't know. I don't know the boy, yet I fear for him."

"Fear for him?"

"He's too different, too innocent and too courageous. He lives in a world of his own and one day someone, something will invade it."

However it was Harold and not Daniel who first attracted scorn.

His absence on the walk to school was often mentioned by the other boys. But Daniel explained that he walked with his brother who had to catch an early train. The village lads accepted this for there was a culture of family loyalty and it was no slight on them if Daniel chose to accompany his brother.

However Harold's aloofness and sense of superiority irked many of his former friends and they began to call him in front of Daniel.

Eventually Daniel snapped at Larry Collins: "You really are being stupid."

There was a sudden silence among the Milford lads as Larry's black eyes turned cold. "You're talking more and more like your bloody brother," he said.

The confrontation had been building up for so long that Daniel was glad to escape into rage. "You don't know anything about either of us really," he said. "Just your stupid little bigotries. That's all."

Larry had no idea what "bigotries" meant but he knew an insult when he heard one. "Oh aye." His eyes were gleaming with anger now. "I'm thinking you're both a couple of posh softies. Just cos your dad has a bit of land."

Daniel was 18 months younger and six inches shorter than the collier's lad but the wind of his rage carried him forward to Larry whirling stinging punches all the while so that the bigger boy, not used to having his reputation treated with such scant respect, was forced to step back without landing a blow of his own. For seconds the others believed that the unbelievable might happen and that Larry Collins might go down, but fast though Daniel was his smaller frame lacked power and gradually the older boy lost the numbing fear of defeat and regained his poise.

He began to stick out his left fist, fast and straight just as his dad had taught him in the many painful sessions at the back of the house. Daniel however moved with the balance of an animal, and though untrained he ducked most of the blows with ease. A good fight looked in prospect until Larry connected with a blow to the ribs that slowed Daniel down. From then on there was only one winner and the exhilaration of Daniel's rage was replaced by the numbing pain of certain defeat as Larry closed his ground. Daniel went down three times before the other lads stepped in.

Tommy McGrath said enough was enough and Larry was quick to agree, for in truth he was beginning to panic at being faced by such a determined opponent. He grinned hugely. He was as generous as a winner as he was mean as a loser and on the way home that afternoon as he and his friends hovered outside his home he admitted that Daniel had given him his hardest fight.

Daniel's esteem went up with all the boys in the village after that but the incident had upset him. He began to spend more time on his own and take long walks into the country. He was happiest there as his wild imagination carried him further than the walk itself.

He still accompanied Harold to the station and as the days passed he began to realise that his brother had problems of his own at the Royal. In the village he was the exception. He was 'the boy at the Royal', the first in the village ever to achieve such status, but at the Royal he was just another scholarship boy, a class of person who was looked down on by some of his fellow pupils. The situation only strengthened his resolve to work harder and to excel. His pride was such that he found it hard to talk about this aspect of his life even to his brother.

One morning as they approached the red brick station the image of the school leapt into his mind. "Of course some of the chaps are very decent," he told Daniel. "Even though they're very grand."

"And yet they are your friends aren't they?"

Harold sighed. Daniel was so innocent at times. "Well you know, I spend a lot of time with them at school and that sort of thing," he said gently.

"But they are not your friends? Real friends?"

Harold found Daniel's stare off-putting as he considered the proposition. "There are some I like. Yes, genuinely like, though we only meet at school. But there are others who act so superior. They are such fools, some of them too." Harold's voice went cold with anger.

Daniel smiled. "Perhaps they fear you, fear your cleverness."

So Harold took to his books and Daniel took to his walking.

Daniel could not understand how everyone seemed so

full of belief when he himself could ask so many questions of a single sentence.

There were consolations from his confusion. Sometimes during a walk a feeling of great beauty would sweep through him overwhelming him until he started to sob and from the first feeling of the beauty to the last of his sob not a word passed through his head. Words were not needed and this filled him with a sense of rejoicing.

At times he despised people for the way they accepted things so easily. He envied them the comfort of their beliefs. Even Harold and all his studying seemed false. His brother accepted so much the order of things, so much information as fact because it was in a book, and all the while he was so lofty with it.

Daniel tried to mock him. "You'd believe the world was square if you read it in a book," he said cuttingly.

"Oh really!" Harold laughed and lounged against the wall by the fire. "And why should you say that eh?"

"It's the way you view everything. You just would. Your mind is like blotting paper."

"Nonsense!" Harold laughed again and felt into his pocket for a notebook. "I accept that memory is only part of intelligence." He thumbed through the book enraging Daniel with his casualness.

"You haven't imagination," Daniel insisted.

Harold looked up from the book. "Daniel you're just being wild. You're throwing as many stones as possible in the hope that one will hit."

He returned the book to his pocket and watched Daniel's face with quiet superiority.

It enraged Daniel to see Harold assuming himself to be special because he had a good memory and an aptitude for study. He thought his own brain was like mercury and Harold's was like a sponge.

"Study is not just the matter of digesting a string of facts; it's about making deductions from them." Harold dealt the killer blow effortlessly.

Daniel lapsed into silence. He almost always lost these confrontations for Harold had the superior weapons for such conflicts. However, privately Harold recognised his brother had different qualities and an innocence that he thought very fine.

Daniel was not sure enough of himself to be so generous with his brother. He believed that Harold did not wrestle with learning but sought refuge in it.

"You don't ask questions Harold. You only think you do." Daniel looked coolly at his brother across the kitchen table one morning. From the corner of his eye he could see their mother through the window as she hung out the washing.

Harold smiled. "Oh, and what don't I ask?"

Daniel hesitated, catching up with his extempore attack. "You only ask superficial questions. You accept things as they seem."

What specifically, Daniel? Name something man."

But Daniel was already speaking of things he could not grasp with clarity. His memory did not compare with Harold's and his brother began picking him off until his confusion turned to anguish.

Thus Harold won though Daniel was the more convinced that he was right, without being any nearer to knowing what right was.

Once Harold sensed Daniel was about to mount an attack and struck first himself.

"And what do you know anyhow?" He asked.

"How can I answer that?" Daniel shrugged.

Harold smiled. "I grant you you read a great deal. But one never hears or sees the outcome of it." He raised his arms to quell Daniel's protest. "Oh I know you believe it all to be so inconclusive. But..."

He cut into Daniel's defences so easily that he stopped out of a sense of guilt.

5

The following summer Edith took the boys on the village's annual picnic. Jud told them that he was too busy to join them, which was as true as it was convenient, for while it was one of his busiest times of the year, he also disliked the outing because he felt trapped in the occasion.

The irony was that on the two years when he could not escape he'd found that he enjoyed the day out. However it was not in his nature to participate in something that he could not leave whenever the mood took him.

Edith made only a token objection to Jud's proposed absence because she feared that he would mock what he called her "vicar's voice."

She did, she admitted, speak slowly and carefully when in the presence of the Reverend Martin but Jud's mimicry of her affectation was a gross distortion. It had got to the stage that he only had to grin when she was in the vicar's presence for the boys to start giggling and for her to feel self conscious.

Harold and Daniel were up at six on the morning of the picnic. Harold was polishing his rough-soled boots when Jud came down with a towel slung over his bare shoulders. Daniel looked at his father's huge frame in awe. As Jud stood with his back to the light his tanned chest was as dark and as thick as a tree trunk.

"Well lads where's me watter?" he boomed. Jud hitched his broad leather belt as he strode across the kitchen and without waiting for reply dug his hands into the sink and splashed the cold water over his head. He spluttered happily as he slapped his damp hands over his chest and armpits.

To Daniel he seemed so strong that he could never die, yet as the boy looked at him Daniel knew that there had been some imperceptible change in his father since yesterday and so it would go on until suddenly something would happen; he would stand in a certain light, or perhaps at a certain angle, and he, Daniel, would be aware of a change.

The boy turned to the kitchen mirror and studied his own smooth face. Old age or even manhood seemed so far away it didn't exist despite the certainty that he would eventually face it and his children after him.

In the larger context, life in the house would be like that. Time was bound to bring about some great event that would pick them up, so that the life they knew now, and accepted with the confidence of routine, would become just a memory.

Daniel smiled to himself. Ironically it was at times like these that time seemed to stand still. That morning he took in the picture of his father and committed it to memory for life as Jud stood shadowed in the window with the sun behind him making the drips of water flash like diamonds on his giant body.

Jud was happy. A whole day's tasks rose before him. His life was moving on with unthinking serenity.

There was a final flurry of his face in the water and then he was up, jerking his head vertical and rasping the towel across his chest and shoulders. The boys watched this performance in silent awe. At last it was over and Jud, his body fresh and alive from the challenge of the cold water, was preening himself in front of the mirror. He pulled on his shirt and picked up his bait tin. "Have a nice day, lads. Tell your mum I had to hurry off." He gave them a huge wink, ruffled their hair with easy affection as he told them: "Don't let the vicar get you down eh." He gave another conspiratorial wink and was off, whistling down the path as they laughed. They loved their father in this mood, and then he'd change like the weather and drift out of their lives again. Even Edith had to smile at some of his antics when he crept up behind her like a kitten tickling her waist with his huge fingers until she squirmed and scolded him.

"Get away you daft man." She cried out, but he only grinned and tickled her some more as the boys' laughter grew louder and louder.

"You're a child Jud Lawson I do declare." She tried to resist his infectious good humour as her hands smoothed the apron over her long dark dress.

Edith heard Jud whistling as he left the house that

morning and it pierced through the last of her sleep. She loved picnic days and their like. Occasion days, she called them; days where nothing else mattered but the day itself and the people around her during it. The event took over from everything and suspended them in time.

She dressed, hurriedly at first, and then spent a few extra seconds sorting herself out, touching up the odd frill in her lace blouse and straightening a crease in her skirt. At last, satisfied, she walked downstairs.

"Did you not have enough sense to light the fire?" she asked the boys, annoyed at being the last up. "Did neither of you think to get some eggs?" She clucked her tongue in disbelief. The boys knew that she was often possessed by dark moods early in the day and waited for it to subside. But there was mischief in Daniel that day.

"How does God judge one, mother?"

Harold's ears pricked up at Daniel's use of the word "one".

"What on earth do you mean Daniel?" Edith snapped at him.

"Well does he judge you as you behave in the morning, in the afternoon, or at teatime?"

"Or at any other time, and are the rules always the same eh?" Harold chimed in. "And does he allow you for aggravation, and if so how does he decide what constitutes aggravation as opposed to natural surliness?"

She searched their faces for trickery and said: "Well this is aggravation indeed. Now get along boys or I'll box your ears." Then she added triumphantly. "And then you'll both be surly won't you."

Both Daniel and Harold began to laugh and she shook her head. "I don't know what gets into you. I don't." She turned away to hide a smile that was creeping from her lips.

By the time she left the house she was as cheerful as the boys and as she carried the basket of food down to the village she spent her time pointing out the birds and wild flowers. A swallow flashed overhead swinging and turning so that the sun caught the white on its wings.

"Look mother, it's caught the snow!" Daniel cried out.

"Don't be silly boy," Edith said laughing.

"Oh mother you're so literal." Daniel laughed in delight.

The Reverend Martin was too big, too booming for the

boys, especially on public occasions. He was conscious that all eyes were on him and this played to his self conceit, so when he spoke he made sure all would hear him. He had gathered his flock outside the church by the time Edith and the boys appeared in the main street and, like all good shepherds, he was concerned the most with those who were furthest from him, even if they were moving in his direction.

"Aaaah Mrs Lawson. Welcome maam. A pleasure. Really," he called over the crowd. Thus they were summoned and they came. The Reverend Martin leaned down and tweaked Daniel's ear. "And your boys too eh. Capital!"

Daniel put his defences up and answered the vicar's inquiries with a series of polite but brief responses. Harold was more guileful and he asked the vicar how his fishing had been, knowing this was his favourite pastime.

He saw his mother's eyes start because only last week he had asked her how a Christian could kill for sport.

Edith had been so alarmed that her son could attack such a pillar of the community that she had answered wildly. "It's in nature boy," she had said. "And anyway it doesn't hurt them." She knew that they were both capable of using their education to trip her up and before they could counter she used her authority. "Your father wants some help in the far field," she said, all too aware of how lame she sounded.

About twenty families had gathered for the outing. The women carried large baskets with crisp linen over them to keep the flies from the food. Almost all of them had baked the previous night and the pleasing scent of fresh bread hung heavy in the air. The families rode in two hay wagons, chatting, laughing and occasionally singing as they followed the river road into the hills.

The Reverend Martin sat in the in first wagon joining in all the songs with his loud, deep voice and delighting all the mothers with his attention to them.

One of the miner's sons, Harry Johnson, had narrowly escaped drowning in the Coquet last year so the vicar had decided to look for quieter waters this summer.

Daniel sat next to Harold with most of the other children in the second wagon. Their backs were pressed against the wooden sides of the wagon and their feet scudded in the thin carpet of hay. Daniel, who had been silent for most of the journey, gave a sudden laugh and whispered to Harold. "Mother won't let you go near Catherine this afternoon after the way you frightened her with the fish."

Harold blushed. His mother swept away his girlfriends like dust from the door and Catherine had been a secret, or so he thought.

Daniel read his brother's mind. "Don't worry, he said, delighted to have Harold off balance for once, "I don't think she suspects anything."

"It's the mother-son thing," said Harold trying to get back on home ground.

"I doubt mother will see it like that," Daniel laughed. "She thinks she's protecting you until you're old enough to look after yourself." Daniel looked impishly at his brother who shrugged and looked away hoping to end the conversation.

But Daniel was enjoying himself too much to allow that.

"But of course such days never come." He winked.

"Oh don't go on so," Harold looked away again and Daniel leaned back content.

The wagon was rocking over the rough tracks now, making the girls giggle. Daniel looked out across the broad sweep of the fields. He found the girls' laughter artificial and so much sillier than his dreams and his thoughts in solitude. He pretended to sleep to avoid conversation. When at last he opened his eyes the road was shadowed by an avenue of elm trees. He stared into the overhang watching the moving mosaic of the leaves against the sky. The chatter of the girls spilled round him and he felt strange, as though he were alone and the others were just creatures in a dream; one of his dreams. He wished he was alone, even from Harold, even from his mother.

The wagon shuddered again, breaking his thoughts. There was another gust of giggles and Daniel saw Catherine's foot roll out with the jerk of the wagon and strike Harold's leg. She talked loudly to the other girls but gave herself away with quick looks at Harold.

Harold pretended not to notice but Daniel could feel the tension in him. Catherine was talking about making a new dress and how she intended to sew the pleats at the front. Daniel studied her with detachment. She had straw blonde hair and a red face because she refused to wear the large hats favoured by some of the other farm girls. Her nose was pert, her blue eyes passive and her voice shrill and loud. Daniel couldn't understand what Harold saw in her. Perhaps he merely liked the fact that she liked him. No, he rejected this out of hand. Harold was not that weak or vain. He wondered whether one came to a stage in life where one was mesmerised, and continued in a state of bliss oblivious to the fact that you seemed absurd to everyone else. Then one day, like his father and mother, you woke up. Or perhaps sometimes you never woke up and the absurdity went on and on. He knew he was too sensitive and that was why the courtship rites of Harold and Catherine put him on edge. His brother, normally so serious, suddenly seemed artificial. He turned to Harold who was affecting an air of nonchalance as he sucked a blade of grass. His right leg lay stretched an agonising inch from Catherine's foot. Neither of them moved and Daniel sensed that both of them were locked together by some strange, exquisite pain. It was as though both of them were conscious that the journey to their little love story would be better than the arrival...that once their feet touched the sensation derived from it would only be diminished by repetition.

Daniel felt a sudden sense of loss. He knew that he and Harold were further apart than at any other time and he sensed that they would only continue to move further away from each other. He remembered the days when they had roamed the countryside unthinking, playing their games and fighting out their squabbles. He regretted their passing just as a child he had regretted the death of Santa Claus; there was a sense of loss that something that had been so dear was gone and would never return.

He was brought from his thoughts by the booming voice of the vicar from the leading cart. "Almost there ladies and gentlemen. Almost there."

Daniel sighed. "I think I could actively dislike that man. He's so patronising to us and obsequious to the gentry."

Harold looked to the vicar who had now broken into song again.

"He got a good degree. He's an Oxford man you know."

Daniel stared at his brother in astonishment. "There are times when I despair for you Harold."

Harold grinned "Just smoking you little brother. You

wouldn't last long as a fish."

Daniel ignored his brother's jibe.

Harold, he knew, was steeling himself to break away from the family. He was neither as hard or as harsh as he liked to make out so when the moment came he would do it clumsily, fighting his emotions until they overflowed and became too blunt. His mother would cry to keep him, cry to make him feel guilty and then cry genuine tears when he finally went away. The thought filled Daniel with gloom.

When the wagons halted in a glade by the river the women draped their linen to make tablecloths on the grass. He waited until they had laid out the food and drink and ate quickly so that he could disappear before the vicar began to organise games. Some of the men had brought beer in thick, cool, stone jars and he slipped away to the edge of the trees as they poured out their drinks. The vicar began to gather the children for a game of tag and hide. "Now then young uns," the great voice boomed out as Daniel trotted deeper into the wood. He took a tighter hold of his handkerchief into which had wrapped some buns and a pasty. Suddenly he felt free of them.

He walked along by the stream until the banks widened and the water became shallow. He looked about him with an expert eye. Across the water some sand martins had dug a nest. He knew better than to thrust his arm into the hole to feel for eggs; the birds always buried them too deep. Daniel splashed across the stream and crouched on the bank above the hole.

He reached for one of the buns and tore off a piece of bread which he flicked down the hole. There was a chirp of alarm. He rolled more pellets and sent two more down to the nest before laying the remainder around the hole. Then he moved quietly down stream, leapt the water and moved up opposite the nest hole.

His day was made now. He would lie there silent and still until a bird came out and then...well, he would watch the neat little thing peck at the crumbs and flee back home. He rested flat on his belly and put a hand under his chin.

The sun was warm in this windless place and he ate his sandwiches before the cheese began to sweat. He did not know how long he had lain there as he drifted in and out of sleep amid the soothing sound of the trickle of the shallow water.

Then he heard the girl's giggle rise sharp into the air. Even as he swung round he knew the laughter was not for him or at him. He was irritated that anyone should come to this secluded spot and yet the laughter drew him. There was another giggle, deeper throated than the first, and this was followed by a lower and more urgent voice of a male. It was Harold.

Daniel crawled quietly up the bank and lay with his head just above the brow. Ahead of him stood half a dozen huge oaks about thirty yards apart but so large were their branches that they covered the sky giving the light beneath them a private, secret quality. The grass was short and brown because the oaks had first won the battle for the light and then the struggle for water.

The voices came again, from the left. Daniel was drawn to them, partly because of the atmosphere of the place and partly because he knew that Harold and Catherine were meant to be a secret. He crawled towards the sound and remained hidden behind the bank. He saw them standing near the last oak.

Harold had taken off his jacket and it lay curled like a sleeping cat unnoticed. They were facing each other a foot apart, tense as though neither could advance or retreat; caught in a web of desires and doubts. But she had the greater resolve. Daniel could see that even from the way they stood, and when Harold spoke it was though she had driven the words from him.

"May I touch you there?" His hand moved towards her breast.

She looked perter than ever in her white blouse. He was the taller and she stretched upwards towards him, raising her breasts. She said nothing, but there was something in her look and her stance that was demanding he did what he had asked. His right hand moved to her and hovered an inch from her breast. Still she stayed looking into his eyes, challenging him, as his hand glided gently as a swan over one breast and then the other. His fingers flicked at the buttons of her blouse and he pulled her breasts from her bodice. His hands were urgent and crushing now but his desire was too fast for her sense of modesty and she broke from the spell like someone jerking from sleep.

She stayed kissing him but her hands gave up grasping him to defend her breasts. They continued like this for at least a minute before Harold broke to the surface of his deep passion.

"What's the matter?"

"I don't want to go further Harold." There were tears in her eyes now and the watching Daniel felt for the second time that day that the world had stopped. They stepped apart and stood like hesitant dancers after a wild reel wondering what to do next now that the music had stopped.

Daniel broke free from them and crawled away

He was full of guilt for weeks. In his sensitive world he esteemed open behaviour because he instinctively believed it to be right.

Through a coincidence of circumstance, innocence and weakness he had felt the guilt of the voyeur. He recognised that the darker qualities within him had ruled over his sense of right and wrong. He refused to sublimate and he felt a sweep of shame pass through him.

6

Within two years Daniel and Harold had both left school. Harold had also left home. His mother fought to keep him but it was a battle she could never win. Even she recognised that later. His education, his training had made his departure inevitable. Harold's ambition had to take him beyond the village if he was to fulfil the dreams she had for him. So when Harold's headmaster arranged for him to take articles with a firm of solicitors in Newcastle the matter was settled.

That Harold seemed destined to become a lawyer filled Edith with awe. At the same time Jud still maintained he could work the farm on his own for most the year so Daniel found himself work with Mr Meredith on his large holding up the valley.

He started work at six each morning and ended the same time each evening. His hours were no longer than Jud's and he earned fifteen shillings a week.

Harold wrote home every weekend. The letters arrived every Tuesday morning and were left on the kitchen table unopened until Jud arrived from the fields. The family assembled after Jud had stamped the dirt out of his boots and taken a hard brush to his trousers. "Came did it?" He asked as he moved towards his waiting sink of cold water. He splashed his face, rubbed himself with a rough towel, and took his chair with his back to the window. Finally he lit his pipe and opened the letter. No one spoke until then. It was as though the ritual of it carried them all along and there was no need to speak.

Both Edith and Daniel could read aloud at talking speed and thought nothing of it but Jud was proud of his own stumbling attempts as neither of his parents had even been able to read their own names.

There many times during these Tuesday evenings that his warm rich voice faltered and Edith and Daniel waited

45

impatiently for him to continue. But they never once objected for they knew that to cut him on such a point would wound him deeply.

Daniel also knew that it was not just the reading that gave Jud pleasure. He was a man who was comfortable with his own lack of determination and drive, choosing to believe that Harold was himself as he might have been and the reading of the letters strengthened that belief.

Gradually those Tuesday evenings became the focal point of the week for the family. They were all together again in spirit as Harold painted his pictures of life in the town.

His first letter described the city as a wondrous place with streets of mighty buildings with tall facades. "It bustles with vigour which I, as a stranger, find exciting, but which they take for granted. I walk the street whenever I can. Sometimes I go to the quayside and watch the dockers bawling and cursing as they swing out their loads on rope cranes near the High Level Bridge over which the old Queen used to travel on her royal train to Balmoral and where the huge steam ships bustle about the river coming and going to all parts of the world. My friend Bennett told me that only a few years ago one hundred thousand people would line the banks of the river to watch sculling races. Imagine that! One hundred thousand people!

Sometimes I stroll to the better end of the town where the ladies glide about like yachts in their long dresses and where the gentlemen raise their hats to everyone.

There is however a large area between these two extremes and it is here, I fancy where the real heart of the city lies; in the swirl of the crowd on busy afternoons, the clatter of the horses and carriages, the presumptuous tooting of the new motor vehicles. Everyone is in a rush to go who knows where; perhaps it is to the shops, to the cafes to the music halls or to the pubs. And on Saturdays there are the football matches of course. Newcastle United play in black and white stripes and consequently are nicknamed the Magpies. They have a huge following and win everything. People say they are the greatest team ever but I would not judge them, knowing so little about the game."

Jud's eyes looked up at this point. "Sounds very exciting don't it"

Edith nodded in agreement. Daniel's eyes never wavered

from a fixed point on the floor.

Harold began to describe his own life. He had a little attic flat in one of the grand houses to the north of the town. The suburb was called Jesmond and was close enough to the city centre for him to walk to and from the office.

Harold's employer, Mr Ormsby, was described as "a most likeable man, a merry, Mr Pickwick of a man. He has two large sideburns which are of course hopelessly out of fashion. He caught me looking at them one day as he took me to court to show me the ropes. He boomed out: 'Lawson, hairstyles and fashion is like morality, a time and a place. These sideburns shall remain in this place until either they are in fashion once more or I am no more.' He asks me questions such as: 'Do you support the Labour Party Lawson? I don't mind at all just so long as you don't bore me with it.' He is quite brilliant in court of course and a gentler, kinder man you couldn't hope to find.

"He believes the world is in too much of a hurry, pushing us from crisis to crisis. The Suffragettes, the Irish Question, Germany's envy of our Empire. He says we all want to right wrongs in a week and so run a greater risk of disaster."

Jud shook his head in an attempt at gravity. "Aye, he'll be right on that you know."

Daniel shook his head gloomily. He instinctively tried to exclude any such problems from his mind, seeing them as essentially man-made and therefore artificial.

As the letters came week after week they built up a picture of his life in the city. Most of Harold's friends were the sons of the wealthy; most of them had been to university and were at least two years older but Harold was far from overwhelmed.

"I am working hard," he wrote. "I spend at least two hours each evening at my table in my room and I am progressing quickly. You would not believe the pleasure I get from study, from knowledge, from understanding. There are some nights, after working hard, where I pace the floor in my excitement. It is a wonderful feeling to be so near to yourself, like dancing in your dreams."

He described his work at the office and said of his colleagues: "By and large they are a decent bunch. There is one chap called Selby who is a bit snobbish but it will pass, I am sure, just like it did at the Royal."

Daniel smiled to himself. He knew Harold's tactics. He would find Selby's beliefs and enthusiasms just as he had done with awkward boys at the Royal and then, when he was ready, he'd attack with controlled and pre-organised arguments, attack with a quiet monotone that he had for such occasions as he probed the weakness of the other's arguments. Then, when Selby had taken one backward step, as Daniel knew he would, Harold would move the talk to something else, as though the whole conversation had been extempore and inconsequential. He'd confronted Harold on the tactic once and his brother had laughed. "I know it's not fair but it's good fun, especially if they're pompous."

Jud had put down the letter. "Hmm," he said. "It seems our Harold is going to make a name for himself they way he's going on."

Edith rose from her chair to look into the pot in the oven by the fire. "It was always obvious that he would, Jud." She never allowed her husband to make an observation about Harold to stand on its own. Even if she merely agreed, she always said something. She stirred the stew. "I only hope he makes some good friends in the city."

Jud dismissed her worries as he had when Harold was at the Royal School. "He'll come out on top will Harold," he said. "It's just in him," and his voice was deep with confidence.

"Aye well." Edith sniffed. "I only hope you're right."

And it seemed that he was. As the letters continued it became apparent that Harold had made three friends, Selby who patted him on the back one afternoon and declared him "up to scratch", Sorrel, a pale fair-haired young man whom Harold said was so innocent that he compelled you to like him and to support him; and Bennett.

Bennett interested Daniel the most, not because of his own qualities, but because when Harold turned to Bennett, his letters lost their smug tone. Indeed it became obvious to Daniel, though not to Jud or even Edith, that Harold held Bennett in awe.

"The other chaps are pretty much as expected," wrote Harold. "Bennett is so different. He is the son of a Bishop and so of course is an atheist. He is quite brilliant." Jud stopped reading, astonished that his son should be meeting with the son of a Bishop. Daniel glanced across to his mother and knew that she would be conveying this information to the Reverend Martin within the day, even if she had to scour the river bank to find him on one of his fishing trips.

Jud returned to the letter after a respectful pause., "Bennett is always discussing things so far from everyday life," wrote Harold. A couple of his friends are aspiring writers and I can honestly say that I have had some of the most interesting times of my life with them." Jud paused again. It was as though he was delivering a sermon and the pause was to emphasise the message which was: Harold, my son, is going to do great things.

He nodded his head slowly in an attempt at solemnity. Daniel noticed his head kept time to the ticking of the old clock that perched on the back window. He turned back to the letter. "Each Friday night we meet at this bar in the town and the talk ranges from poetry to whether or when Germany will start the war. Then when the landlord finally summons up courage to turf us all out (some of us argue very fiercely) we continue under the nearest lamp until, finally we go our separate ways or, more often than not, we end up at someone's lodgings and talk some more. Often there are not enough seats for all of us and we sprawl around on the carpet leaning against the walls. The room is thick with tobacco smoke and the passion of our voices. Sometimes the landlady or landlord objects to the noise but it is all rather grand and fine. Sometimes I wish I was a writer but it is not to be for I have no talent in that respect, of course.

"Bennett too, tried and failed at writing, though that is the only thing I can conceive him failing in for he holds the floor in these debates of ours with such fervour and keenness and you can sense the immediate respect for him every time he speaks. He says that one can only believe in something by first believing in nothing."

Daniel snorted at his brother's tone of reverence remembering how Harold had dismissed similar arguments he had put forward. The letter went on to mention Mr Ormsby. His employer had asked Harold to tea the following Sunday. This was unprecedented among the juniors and Harold was very proud of this honour. All the other indentured staff now regarded him as first among equals.

Jud raised his head from the letter. Daniel was sitting in the far corner of the room and he could see his mother and father at the same time. Both their faces were warm with pleasure and pride. Each time Jud finished reading a letter Edith placed it in a sewing box.

Harold failed to write the following week and a mood of gloom descended over the house. Edith posted a letter to Harold asking him whether he was well. Jud snapped at the least thing. By the time the following Tuesday arrived even Daniel was relieved to see a letter on the table when he arrived home from work that evening. He had spent the day cleaning a ditch in one of the long fields and the mud was caked to him.

He strode upstairs and changed into clean trousers before washing himself at the big sink in the kitchen. As he stood naked from the waist down Edith could not but be overtaken by his beauty. The physical labour had turned his body into a sculpture. He had, she realised suddenly, the unconscious grace of an animal.

She knew too that both her boys had left her. Harold with his intellect and ambition had departed physically and Daniel? He was still with her of course but his mind was moving elsewhere. He no longer looked to her for approval. He'd grown out of her control and in his own quiet but definite way he'd gone in all but body.

Daniel looked at the letter. The address was in Harold's firm hand. The envelope was ripped open. Edith had been unable to wait for Jud. She wanted news of her son.

"He's alright," she said. "He's had a chill but he's alright now."

Jud went straight to the letter when he came in from the fields. He said nothing about the opened envelope but sat in his chair by the window and began to read as though no one knew the news.

"The lad's been ill," he said. "There's been a right carry on. Daft kid."

Harold told them he suffered a chill on the weekend he was due to meet Mr Ormsby. "I did not feel too bad at first and I had no way of warning the family that I could not attend. So after staying in bed all day Saturday I decided that I must at least make the effort of responding to this honour.

50

"However by the time I got to Mr Ormsby's house I was dizzy and damp with sweat. Mr Ormsby took one look at me, told me I was stupid, and had me driven home. I have been in bed for a week and returned to work yesterday. Everyone was most pleasant and Mr Ormsby has invited me for tea the following Sunday. He really is a most understanding man."

The letter went on to give some impressions of the city.

"There are times when it is very lonely," he wrote. "Often one can walk through streets and there is no one that one knows; only the buildings are familiar. However there is also much to do. The theatres, the dancehalls, the music halls and I do now have a wide variety of friends.

Also I love to go for walks in some of the finer parts of the city. Some of the houses are so impressive, so full of character. Selby took me home for tea a couple of weeks ago. His father's house is very grand. There are so many rooms and they are so large and high. He told me they had lived there all his life and each door had its own sound shutting. We sat out on a long lawn among a galaxy of flowers, gladioli, dahlias, roses and so many others. We sipped tea and talked of pleasantries. It was all so stylish, so English."

The letters arrived frequently throughout the following winter and Jud and Edith preened themselves at their son's progress. In one letter Harold complained about Bennett. He appeared to believe in nothing which was all very well except that he seemed to want everybody to do the same.

"There was one day we walked through Jesmond Dene to our flat (I lodge at his house) and he started to mock my ambitions as being ultimately futile. I argued of course and in the end he looked very sad and said: 'I wonder whether either of us will survive the war.' "

Jud put down the letter. "What war?" He asked.

Daniel smiled. "Bennett seems to believe there is going to be a war."

Jud shook his head and returned to the letter.

"Bennett is always harsh on young Sorrel," Harold wrote. "He will brook no interruption from him and scorns his questions. There is a writer called Norman Angell who believes that there can be no war because all the likely parties are economically bound up with each other. Sorrell just happened to ask a few of us as we strolled home: 'Have you read Angell?' It was more to make conversation than anything else but Bennett snapped back: 'Of course. Everyone has read Angell.' And then he proceeded to tear the theory to pieces. I felt sorry for Sorrel. He's such a nice chap. I hope you'll meet him one day. Bennett says he is not nice. It is just his lack of confidence that makes him appear so. I don't agree. There are times when Bennett is at odds with his colleagues. He broods a lot too. He is convinced that there will be a war within the year.

"As though to back his words we came across an angry crowd as we walked past a butcher's shop on the way home. The trader is called Kruger. He's a harmless chap but some of the crowd had broken his shop window and they were shouting things at him; that he ought to be a pork butcher because he was a filthy German pig.

"All the while the poor fellow was hiding behind his shop door shouting 'But gentlemen I was born here. In Ashton Street. Number 23. Number 23.' In the end the constables came and moved the crowd along though I don't believe anyone was charged. Mr Kruger's son, a boy aged about ten I guess, saw the whole scene from an upstairs window. He was sobbing his heart out. The whole thing was most upsetting. Such ignorance allied to such ill temper is both frightening and depressing."

Jud shook his head sadly. He regarded Harold's letters unquestioningly as a true and complete record of the outside world. "I hope this chap Bennett and our Harold are wrong," he said.

Daniel stayed silent. He refused to speak about the war. He had seen the young men of the village enjoy such talk as they sat on their haunches and bragged to each other that they would like to get the chance to give "them Germans" a lesson. Some had the decency to glance about with a flicker of self consciousness.

Jud talked in simple dogmas about the Germans. They were, he said, jealous of our empire. Sometimes Edith rescued Daniel from such conversations. "Empires," she said in her cutting tone. "Empires. What do you know about Empires? Your empire only stretches to the King George." But more often than not Daniel was forced into an argument with his father who heard only the echoes of his own mind.

In contrast Daniel thought that he would give anything just

for one day in which his confused thoughts focussed with blinding light on a clear truth. Instead, however, he struggled amid blurred theories.

At times the letters created a feeling of sadness. He saw his mother and father nodding their heads in approval at Harold's record of self advancement and yet he found he was getting another picture from the letters; that Harold's triumphs were self defeating because they were fought out amid a background of emptiness and loneliness. Harold had friends, he had colleagues, but among the swirl of all those people he had no community and Daniel knew that the village boy in his brother would miss that, no matter how he tried to hide the fact from himself with his grand phrases and designs.

There were times as Jud's deep voice filled the room that Daniel felt himself an outsider in the home.

Then one week Harold mentioned a girl he had met at some function and he saw some hope for his brother. She must have been important for Harold to have written of her. He knew the mention of this girl was but an opening gambit and that more about her would follow. He was so certain of this that a vision of her jumped into his mind. She was pretty with dark hair. She and Harold were dancing slowly on a smooth lawn and they were smiling. Her clothes were beautifully cut and she glided in her dress. They were dancing to music that came through the open windows of a large house. Suddenly it stopped and so did they. Daniel remembered the girl in the forest and he realised how far Harold had travelled.

7

Daniel found life very different on the big farm. He had been used to working alone or with his father in the small fields, or with a few helpers during harvest. But Mr Meredith's farm swarmed with hands especially at the harvest of hay or wheat, or when the potatoes and turnips were to be picked, or the fields cleared of stones ready for the next sowing. Many of the workers were women. They worked in wide skirts and wide hats which were held down with scarves. The hats protected the skin from the sun. Often there were nearly forty people in one big field working with the hay sweeps and building up the stacks until they were larger than the average cottage.

The girls got more than their fair share of the dirty work, Daniel thought. In a corner of one of the central fields Mr Meredith had a huge manure heap with aisles leading into it. Every so often the girls had to walk down the aisles with pitchforks turning over the muck. Daniel could smell the manure from fifty yards down wind so he didn't like to dwell on what it must be like for the lasses.

Some of the girls were the daughters of miners who took on the job for some quick money in the summer. Others were the daughters of farm workers who just drifted into the fields for want of something else to do.

Daniel and the others assembled in the big farmyard each morning unless they already knew their work for the day.

On Saturdays he walked to the village with the miners' girls but if they had been turning muck they shooed him away for many of the lads mocked them over the smell and it offended their femininity even though they were bustling, raucous girls.

The labouring was hard work and there was no romance in it. But he needed its simplicity for he found that easy to accept and in that state of grace he was rewarded with a sense of wonder. This remained with him during all his time on the land, even after the sunny days of the harvest were over and he was bending in the autumn drizzle looking for stones in bleak fields, or when he spent days planting potatoes.

The girls took to him from the first day. They made no secret that they found him attractive though at that time he had just turned seventeen. When their numbers made them bold and they wanted mischief they called to him giggling. When they saw that this made him embarrassed they became bolder.

Sometimes they went too far and became ridiculous as when Beth Chadwick stood by the side of the manure heap one day as he passed and invited him to "lie in Mr Meredith's hay".

Early in the spring of 1914 Daniel witnessed a scene he carried with him for the rest of his life. He was strolling towards the village with some of the farm girls and as they reached the rise he looked down the valley road. A group of miners were walking slowly toward Milford carrying a bundle on an old door. He knew it was heavy because he could see the tiredness in their shapes; then they disappeared behind the alder and poplar trees that lined the road. Suddenly one of the girls, Susan Moody, gave a shriek of horror as they reappeared. Daniel saw that all the men had taken off their flat caps and he felt a stab of alarm as Susan started to run down the slope. The other girls picked up her panic like a flock of birds and in an instant all of them were racing over the fields. Then Daniel knew what they already knew; that the bundle on the door was a body and the girls were racing to account for their fathers, their brothers and their husbands. They called out in alarm and fear as they raced down to the village and the alders and the poplars flitted this way and that revealing and then hiding the tiny figures as they trudged along the road. As the girls got closer they called out the names of their loved ones, some in recognition, some in entreaty and still the alders swayed in the wind so the brothers and fathers must have lived and died many times in the hearts of the girls.

Daniel caught up with them just as the men reached the other end of the village. He heard their thick studded boots scud on the road. By now people were rushing from their houses, the first because they had seen the men or heard the cries of the girls and then the rest as they picked up the alarm that had passed through the village like electricity.

The women were wailing in a strange communal dirge. Someone called out. "It's Jimmy Morgan. The shaft caved in."

They'd not washed him and Jimmy Morgan lay as still as stone on the door. Some blood had run from his mouth and congealed on the coal dust that covered his face. Mrs Morgan was in the street screaming. Her apron fluttered slightly as her tiny frame knelt over the body. Her hands were covered with flour and they left an imprint on her husbands face as she stroked him. The miners stood back from her out of respect. Their dark, set faces were full of tiredness as they stood caps in hands round the body. A tear slivered like a white worm down the coal ingrained face of one of the men. Daniel pushed himself to a good vantage point. He found himself pulled to the tragedy; he wanted to say something and yet, at the same time, realised there was nothing to say. Words were useless.

Susan Moody stumbled on a stone and he caught her as she fell. She clung to him and he was glad to feel her warmth even though he was stiff with tension.

A neighbour began to comfort Mrs Morgan. She pulled her head to her and murmured sounds that mothers make to babies. All the women were weeping now. One of the women stepped forward and covered Morgan's face with a white tea towel. It was a cathartic moment, a moment of grace. The white towel seemed to suggest to Daniel that the man was at least at peace. He took comfort from it. Then he felt Susan's body warm and soft on his arm and he noticed the sleeve of his rough shirt was damp with her tears. He felt a sudden tenderness.

The village was full of rumours now. "It was a truck that got him," someone said. Then Mr McQuinn, the husband of the woman who had brought Daniel into the world said: "Truck or what. It doesn't matter. All the bastards gave us was an old door to carry him home. He was a union man see."

The men fell silent at this and one of the women whispered: "At least they've got no bairns. Not like Michael McCann," referring to a miner who had died two years gone.

Then, just as Daniel was wondering how they would all move on from here, one of the men leaned forward and took a gentle hold of Mrs Morgan

"Best get Jim inside." The miner spoke softly and the idea was taken up by the others. Four of them picked a corner each of the door and they advanced slowly on the cottage. Their progress was easy enough until they realised that the door was too broad for the doorway. A woman gasped in horror as the men tried to angle the door and the body started to slip on the surface. A miner stepped forward and held the body as the men made their uncertain advance into the house.

Another of the miners broke with the strain. "Is that all the bastards can afford? A door for a dead man," he shouted.

"Not even the colliery cart," shouted another and for a second the men rippled with anger as they found a focal point. Some more called out, their voices high pitched with tension, but others quietened them. Poor Jimmy was dead and that for the moment overrode everything else, even their disgust at the way he had been treated.

The horror of the scene lived with Daniel for many days but there was something else which unsettled him. The incident and the villagers' reaction to it had demonstrated with clarity something he had always feared in his heart; the life in the village was not as self-contained as he would have liked it to be. It was affected by other things over which he had no control. He could not determine the consequences but he sensed they were profound.

The whole village and the workers on the surrounding farms turned out for the funeral and they walked slowly in a long thick file as the tired toll from the church bell rolled up the valley filling every home with its mournful sound. The colliery owner sent a wreath. The men's faces turned hard and cold at the sight of it resting against the coffin.

It was weeks before the village recovered from Jimmy Morgan's death but eventually the quoits came out in the square behind the George and the miners began to play for stakes again.

Daniel got to know all the gossip of the village each weekend when he visited the barber for a weekly shave. It cost a penny but he enjoyed the long warm luxury of having something done for him. During the week Mr Dent cut hair for two pence a go but on Saturdays he would open for shaves as the miners queued for the "close do", anxious to smarten up for Saturday night. Some of them were so fashion conscious that they even wore spats, to the amusement of their friends.

Mr Dent paid a lad a couple of two pence to slap the lather on for him as he moved swiftly from chair to chair saying nothing much else but, "There you are. There you are."

Daniel was fascinated by the miners. He could not understand their desire to work underground, despite the extra shillings. They seemed to have a fierce pride in their job and some of them had no ambitions beyond getting work as a hewer so they could have the privilege of cutting their own coal.

The barber's shop was at the other end of the village from the George and as soon as Daniel had paid his penny he walked to the pub stroking his warm smooth chin. He passed some of the pit wives who stood at their doors gossiping.

They'd all taken a liking to "the farmer's son" and would call to him as he passed.

"Is Bobby in the chair yet?"

"Tell my Frank that if he's not back from the pub soon I'll take his dinner in to shame him."

The other women laughed at this for they all remembered when Edna Williams had done just that and got a hiding from her husband for showing him up in front of his mates. All the same it had been noted that Sam Williams had rarely been late for a meal after that and so some of the other wives would threaten to do the same.

But Daniel laughed at the threat. "He'd only eat it and then continue drinking," he said.

The merriment from the doorways reached right down the street. The wives liked to jibe with Daniel. He was the most striking of youths and he moved with a rare ease that made it easy on the eye just to watch him walk down the street with the sun on him. There was a life and a grace in his movement that was attractive, even after he'd put in a twelve-hour stint in the fields. His body never slumped with tiredness, he had no airs and graces, and he never set up his cheek, unlike some of the lads when they saw the wives nattering at their doors.

8

Harold came home that spring. His letter gave them just two weeks warning which was as well as Edith chattered about nothing else and walked to the village at the least excuse to tell the world about the visit of her son.

She scraped the cottage clean and changed her hairstyle for three mornings running before Harold was due to arrive.

One of the farmers along the valley had killed a pig a week back and she cajoled Jud to buy a leg. When the great day came they were in their finest. Even Jud had polished his boots until they gave off a deep, dark glow. It was a warm morning but Edith had already decided she was going to wear her best coat and that was it.

As they strolled along the lane to Swannell Daniel picked a tiny primrose off a hedge and stuck it in her lapel. Jud said it stuck out nicely against the brown of her coat. They were early for the train of course and when it finally steamed in Harold was last off.

Suddenly he was there, walking through the steam of the engine in his neat dark suit and stiff white collar. He looked round searching for them and then their eyes all met and they all smiled at once.

Edith caught him looking at the primrose. "Daniel picked it from a hedge on the way over." She smiled.

Harold smiled back. "I thought it looked fresh."

Edith laughed. "Of course it's fresh. This is the country you know."

They all laughed and she hugged him slowly. As they walked from the station Daniel caught Harold glancing at them and he wondered what changes he had seen in their appearance. Daniel could only suspect that their mother had more streaks of white in her hair and that their father's skin was harsher and more grizzled about the neck. He was a witness to the daily erosion but Harold's prolonged absence ironically would give him a clearer view of the changes in them. There was a strange formality about them, all in their best clothes. Daniel kept searching for some new event only to realise that they were the event themselves.

His father had a strange, new-scrubbed look. "I hope you are up for walking back," he said turning to Harold who was carrying a small leather suitcase. "Unless the city ways have taken you that is."

"On the contrary," said Harold quickly. "I walk to work every morning and home every evening."

"Aye walking is good for you," said Jud nodding. They chatted happily on the way home. Edith wanted to know the sort of life the ladies lived and Harold smiled and said: "It's very grand. Very grand."

"Oh come on Harold." Edith was all eager like a little girl. "You must tell me more than that."

Harold smiled looking very wise. "Well mother last week I went to a cricket match with Selby and some of the others. I was merely a spectator but Selby was batting for most of the afternoon and at tea time we strolled about. All the ladies were there with their children and their hampers, and everywhere you looked, no matter where, there was not the least bit of haste. Even the children chasing balls seemed to give off a sense of quiet because they were so much part of the pleasant picture. Selby drifted up to my side and said: 'You know Harold, this *is* England.'"

Harold looked about him but no one spoke; they bowed to his authority on such matters to the extent that he found he had to be his own critic also. "Now that may be a silly thing to say but if you had been there you would know what he meant. There was a certain style." He looked at his mother. "Does that answer your question do you think?"

Jud chipped in with a grin. "Of course it doesn't, lad. She wanted a load of names and titles to give to the neighbours."

"Oh Jud really!" Edith was stung by his mockery but Jud, who could feel the boys egging him on, just grinned the more and gave a deep laugh. "Still," he said, "No doubt she'll winkle a few more out of you by the end of the week." They all laughed for they knew Edith had a weakness for such things.

The stone walls of the kitchen were freshly whitewashed

and within their confines hung the heavy, sweet smell of fresh baking. Edith had made half a dozen loaves and a fruit cake in the fire oven. It all brought back happy memories and Harold began to rise to it all. Outside on the walk back he had breathed in the fresh country air and now inside there was the warmth of the baking and the warmth of his family. He was relieved to find himself happy in these surroundings. "It's good to see you," he said suddenly, laughing as though startled by the fact. He squeezed his mother.

"Oh stop it Harold," she laughed. "You're as bad as Jud. You don't know your own strength." She looked at him. He had grown into a fine young man. He had his father's fine features but the look about his eyes was stronger, more confident.

Harold himself tried not to assess them. He and they were living different lives now but they were family, and that was that.

His memories began to spring from the chairs and the walls and the ornaments and the views. It took him a couple of days before he could relax in the silences of the place. Then his mother scolded Daniel one night as his brother scraped his boots at the kitchen door after a day's work in the fields. He took in the old rhythm of his mother's voice and then that of his brother's as Daniel answered her back.

The familiarity grew round him.

"I'll be able to grow spuds in the kitchen at the rate you're spreading muck," Edith scolded him.

"I'll sweep it out in a minute," Daniel pulled off his boots and untied the rough string that kept his trousers hitched above his feet. Then he slapped the dust out of his clothes and put on his shoes that his mother insisted he wore inside. It was one of the little refinements that separated them from the rest of the community.

Daniel's collarless shirt was half open and his waistcoat was undone. There was a sheen of sweat over his smooth brown chest. He walked over to the fire and rolled a paper spill from which he lit his first pipe of the day.

Edith turned to the stew she was cooking. Daniel glanced across at Harold and winked at him and gave a boyish grin. Harold warmed to him and they began to talk.

Harold spoke in much the same tone as he wrote to them

about the style of the city. Daniel allowed him to talk but all the while became increasingly sure that Harold was persuading himself of the enticing grandeur of the place, papering over his own doubts, because this was the only way he could fulfil his ultimate ambitions.

Harold began to talk of Bennett but found Daniel's silence off-putting.

"He's extremely intelligent." He heard the words and realised how pompous he must sound. Then he compounded the error. "In fact," he charged on," he's probably the cleverest person I've met." Harold knew he was being absurd and he was conscious that Daniel was grinning. Edith sensed the discord while stirring the depths of her stew. She turned to them ladle in hand. "Why don't you boys get out from under my feet? Dinner'll be half an hour yet. Why don't you go for a walk?"

Daniel looked across at Harold who nodded. "Why not?" He rose from his father's chair by the window. The two of them moved to the door glad to escape from the atmosphere that was building the cramped room.

They strode towards the hills and suddenly Harold began to feel more at ease, confident even. "You know Daniel," he said. "You really should sort out what you are going to do with your life."

"I have," Daniel said shortly. Neither of them spoke again for a while as they followed the lane that sloped to forest that stood a grey smudge on the high land. "I'm happy here," he said simply.

Harold shook his head. "I can never understand why you don't want to better yourself, or at least involve yourself."

"I am involved. I'm involved here," Daniel swept his hand to the horizon. "And as for bettering myself what does that mean. That I feel better about my life or that I rise in rank and so am thought to be better." He laughed his clear laugh.

Harold shook his head. "But don't you fear being bored in the future and then finding you can't do anything about it? Now is the time to make such decisions."

Daniel just looked at Harold and smiled. Harold felt his face redden. "I know I'm sounding pompous, patronising even. But I'm concerned because I love you."

The evening air was full of velvet. The trees were still as

stone on either side of the lane. A hay cart rested against an oak tree. The path they walked had been worn by the feet of men. Not a leaf moved in the evening air.

Harold gave a short laugh. "You know I am so used to the rumble of the traffic and the cries from the streets that here I hear the silence. It's almost alarming." Daniel said nothing. He had been irritated by his brother's lecturing.

At last Harold spoke again. "Change is part of life. All life is changing at all times. That is why I fear for you. I fear for you because you seem to always be moving on a path of your own and usually against the herd."

It was Daniel's turn to laugh sharply. "And what's wrong with that? History shows that the minority is usually right."

Harold turned to him his eyes, his expression, even more earnest than usual. "I fear for you because you will take everything to excess with your stubbornness. It's dangerous to walk into a stampede."

Daniel laughed again. "Not if the stampede is going straight for a cliff."

"Some of the herd will survive. They always do."

Harold sighed. The fresh air and their heavy talk had made him suddenly tired. He escaped into the sights around him; each landmark was a signpost to his memories.

He knew Daniel better than his brother gave him credit. He felt almost part of him at times and this was one of them.

He too could enjoy the fields, the trees, the hedges and the heavy sky and the sense of wonder that they all belonged to each other. He could half close his eyes, like his brother did and they all blurred into one perfection. And, if pushed, he too would accept that the countryside was one of man's greatest creations, formed by the labour of the farmer who had created a fertile land out of an overgrown wilderness of forest and swamp.

Daniel's voice drifted into his thoughts. "I think we should all learn to live near to ourselves and not gallop off with wild ideas," he said softly.

The words irritated Harold and he sprang from his reverie. "And what does that mean eh? It's one of those things that sound fine until you start to analyse it."

Daniel shook his head. "Harold you understand only the

ways of the world you have chosen. You are in danger of becoming that most rare of things, a boring zealot, because you think your world is the only real world, the only practical world because it is based on power and the ability to defend itself."

"And you could join it if you but choose now. But what is your world at present eh?"

Daniel turned slowly to look out across the landscape. "There are times when I wish I was a bird," he said.

Harold blinked at him in astonishment. "You're not serious are you?" He remembered Daniel had a cunning trick of throwing a stick and watching you run after it.

Daniel did not reply. He walked across the lane and plucked a leaf from the hedge. He stroked it slowly staring at its deep sheen. They'd reached the top of a hill and he turned to stand staring into the hills that lay beyond. At last he spoke. "Sometimes up here when the clouds are low they seem to be lying at the end of the lane and to walk along the lane is to walk off into the sky." He turned to face his brother. "If you could would you?"

Harold laughed, nervous at the strangeness of the question. "What kind of daftness is this?" He glanced at his brother. "You used to say such things as a child."

Daniel shrugged. "It's what I see as an adventure I think."

As Daniel looked towards the pale setting sun Harold was struck by the smooth beauty of his face. Perhaps, he thought, Daniel did not need the stage of life.

"Why try to change me?" Daniel asked. "Why try to make me so similar to you? Are you so certain that your way of life is the only way of life?"

Harold smiled. "No, of course not. I suppose I find it hard to understand you." He glanced at Daniel again. "Do you read all my letters?"

"Dad reads them out every Tuesday."

Harold smiled. "Oh I see. You don't seem to have much regard for what I am trying to do."

"What a strange thing to say. Of course I am interested. But I view them in a different way. I don't look at them in the same way that mum and dad do."

"Oh. What do they say?"

"Oh they're very proud of you. You must never let them

down you know. Not like I do." He gave a short laugh.

"Oh come now!"

"No really! They are very proud of you Harold."

Harold looked gloomily at his polished shoes that had a veil of dust on them now. "It's very difficult in the city you know."

Daniel caught the edge in his voice.

"It's very difficult for me to establish myself. I must be best. That is the least I must do to be accepted. Or I should say the least I expect of myself. It's very difficult."

Daniel noticed Harold's face was slightly heavier since his sojourn to the city. His body like his character was filling out.

"What of the girl you wrote about?"

Harold made a heroic attempt at keeping his voice steady and his effort might have escaped the notice of anyone but his brother. "She is very attractive and her name is Dominique."

"That's a pretty name." Daniel tried to encourage him.

"It is isn't it," Harold smiled. Then after a pause he added: "She's half French." He looked at Daniel once more. "She is," he said at last, "well connected. Her father is a businessman. In shipping."

Daniel smiled mischievously, "Does she know your brother digs ditches?" He laughed. "Do you think she'd mind much?"

Harold shook his head. "I should think not."

"It would be understandable," said Daniel kindly.

Harold stared at him. His face, as ever, was determined but his earnest blue eyes softened with gratitude. "I did something terrible once," he said. "It was when I went to see Mr Ormsby you know. She lives nearby you see and she had been visiting him that day. Well I walked to the next tram stop just in case she should be passing and see me waiting for the tram. I didn't want her to see me doing that."

Daniel shook his head. "That is terrible Harold."

Harold nodded his head. "I felt ashamed. The absurd part is that I do not believe she is remotely like that."

"But you fear that if she was you would just accept it?"

The sun had dropped behind the hills now and the evening was closing in with a sudden chill. Harold's voice was soft and even, that of a man who has come through a trial. "Yes I did fear that once. I have such a lowly position; all I have is my ambition and my energy, and I fear her parents will see me as a bad match. Do you understand that Daniel?"

"Yes. I understand." Daniel smiled. "But never forget that you have ability and determination. Others will see your qualities."

The days passed quickly after that. Harold's mother had accepted his absence by now and had readjusted her life. Sometimes when they were alone in the afternoons she ran out of things to say and she worked on in silence. He felt that the house was waiting for him to leave so that it could slip back into its accustomed routine. He knew too that he did not belong here any longer and they knew it also, so at times they felt they were in limbo as they waited for time to move them back to their accustomed lives.

Harold's life was now in the city. His role in the family was to be a visitor, a loved one, but a visitor nevertheless.

Harold and his father talked of simple things in the evening as they always had. However those little talks left Harold fearing for Daniel whose agile mind had more distant horizons than simple thoughts and commonsense. He feared that his prophesies to Daniel would come true; that one day he would be trapped in these surroundings.

On the Friday night Jud announced that as Harold was now a man he and his son should go down the King George for a night on the beer.

The miners and the farm labourers accepted Harold as Jud's son but there was an undeniable gap between them and the young man and they struggled to find common ground.

"So you've had a right good education then, young Harold," said one of them nodding his head all friendly and his mates did the same.

Harold smiled encouragingly. "I suppose it's a bit like learning a trade," he said.

"Aye," said the friendly miner. "Bettering yourself like." The flat caps nodded again. Harold took the opportunity to buy them a drink at the long wooden bar. But, as they stood around chatting, Harold realised that far from being the watched he was the watcher. He was an outsider now, in his home, and in his village.

The following day he looked on as his father cleared a ditch at the bottom his largest field. Jud was still strong and the spade slung away the dirt with the easy pace of an expert. There was no hurry, no desperate exertion and the job was done without his taking off his dark waistcoat. Harold felt a slight beckoning as he watched the easy rhythm of his father's movement, but that was all.

He left his father with a smile and a word and walked back up the hill along the road that made him ache with memories. His life in the city was the only one that could fulfil him and he needed to escape into the challenge he found there, even though it meant him leaving the three people he loved.

The warmth of the kitchen covered him as soon as he opened the door. His mother was sitting by the fire, rocking gently in her chair as she darned a pair of Jud's rough woollen socks. She had always felt the chill of the evening even in the summer. He rested his hands on her shoulders and squeezed her with affection. "I must go back tomorrow mother," he said simply.

"I know son," she paused in her darning as she spoke.

He looked at her. She was sitting in the light from the fire that was kind to her but he could see the grey in her hair and the skin hanging loose from her throat. He said nothing but squeezed his mother's shoulders a second time and walked over to the window to look down the valley towards the village. The cottages were hidden by the trees that took the edge off the valley wind but he could see the smoke churning from their chimneys and turning to the right he saw his father walking slowly up the long field with his spade over his shoulder like a soldier with a rifle. In the distance the hills swelled up gently behind him. It was a picture that stayed in its time but he knew that time was moving him on, that he could not stay in this community, could not live among its certainties. It was amid the exciting uncertainty of the city that his future must lie even though in moments of self-doubt it could make him ache with loneliness.

He hated goodbyes. They seemed so inadequate. He shook his father and his brother by the hand that night for he knew that they would be in the fields when he left in the morning and it was not enough to say farewell as they gulped at their tea and porridge.

As it was Jud grinned at him over the breakfast table and said: "I know folk look down at porridge nowadays but it seems to me that if you like summat you should eat it, eh."

Harold smiled and nodded, glad to have something as simple and true as this to carry him through his goodbyes. "You must come to see me in Newcastle," he said. His father, his mother and his brother all smiled. But no one answered.

9

That spring three of Farmer Meredith's ewes died giving birth. The surviving lambs were given the coats of others that had died. Two were taken by the ewes but the third was rejected and Meredith was reconciled to losing the tiny beast until Daniel told him of a trick he had heard at one of the markets.

The lamb and the prospective mother were shut away together on one of the top fields. Each evening Meredith and Daniel walked up to take a look at them but each time Daniel said it was too early to try his experiment.

Then, after six days, the light was slipping into the sky as the two of them strode up the hill with Meredith's dog, Lucky, bounding round them in great loops as though he was rounding them up.

The road up the hill was narrow and rutted with cart tracks. Below them lay Milford with all but the tops of the cottages hidden by trees. The plumes of light from the chimneys glowed in the dusk as the women prepared ther evening meals over the kitchen fires. Further up the slope he could see his own home half-hidden by a great elm that his mother loved and that his father threatened to fell every time his mother had the urge to smash his huge mirror. Two fields along a bush drainage trench snaked out like a large finger across his father's land. The work had taken Jud four days and, if he continued at his present rate he expected to finish by the weekend.

The way was getting steeper now and every few strides Mr Meredith would glance at Daniel envying the spring in his young legs.

"Reckon it'll work Daniel?" He'd asked the same question each time they'd walked the slope and each time Daniel had merely given that slow smile of his and shrugged in his easy fashion which Mr Meredith had wit enough to realise was not rudeness merely the way of the lad.

They walked another hundred yards or so and Daniel motioned to some tiny wild roses that fizzed with colour in the dark hedge. "Pretty eh!"

"Aye," said Mr Meredith rubbing the itch at the rim of his hat where the sweat had soaked in. His red face shone with the effort of striding up the slope.

Daniel plucked a blade of grass from the side of the track and sucked heavily on it.

They had come to the rise in the path and Mr Meredith could see at last the field and the stacks of hay which had been used to form a shelter for the beasts.

Daniel looked over the side of the hay stacks. The ewe stared at him mute and passive. The lamb stirred nervously. Daniel turned to Mr Meredith who was looking on impatiently. Get your whistle ready," Daniel said at last.

"You think they're ready then?" the farmer asked unnecessarily.

"Get the dog ready and I'll let them out." Daniel's voice rose with excitement. "Now leave off them for a while until they get their bearings."

Neither of them was conscious that there usual roles were being reversed.

"Right." Mr Meredith pulled the whistle from his pocket and brought Lucky to order.

Daniel leaned forward and then pulled two bales aside and then two more. There was now a clear gap and he stepped back to allow the beasts to escape. The lamb came out first scampering carelessly into the field. The ewe hesitated at this new situation her slow eyes moving in suspicion. Gradually she moved from the pen testing the wind with her nose.

"Shall I let Lucky off?"

Daniel stayed him with a gesture of his arm. "No not yet. It's the ewe that matters."

Mr Meredith fidgeted impatiently and at last Daniel gestured for him to begin. The whistle sounded a shrill quavering note and the dog ran straight for the lamb knocking him over so that the little beast squealed in fear. It got to its feet and started to run towards the ewe but Lucky was much the quicker and he sent the lamb spinning over again. The drama was repeated three or four times more and Daniel and Mr Meredith exchanged anxious glances

The ewe had appeared aloof to the drama and then just as the two men were fearing the worst, the lamb squealed once more. The chord cut deep into the ewe's maternal instincts and it seemed to Daniel that he was witnessing some great truism of life as the ewe moved forward with a deep call of anguish. She ran towards the dog with such persistence that Lucky was forced to give ground. Mr Meredith whistled for the dog to advance slowly on the lamb but the ewe stood her ground.

Then suddenly she charged the dog and Mr Meredith cried out excitedly, "She's taken to the little beast." He waved his hat in the air.

The two men grinned at each other sharing the moment. Then Mr Meredith spoke again. "My God Daniel I tell you there was a moment there when I wouldn't have put a farthing found in a ditch on it. But we've done it lad, or I should say you've done it. For truth to tell I've never seen the like before."

Daniel smiled. "Aye it was a close call in the end. Perhaps we should have left them together for another day?"

"No lad you got it perfect." The farmer shook his head in wonderment. "Never seen the like. Never seen the like." He patted Daniel on the back. "Well done lad. Tell me just then. How did you know?"

Daniel grinned. "I just did."

10

The bar was half full when Daniel arrived at the George. There was the odd labourer from the farms, some with their boots and clothes still covered in dust, mingling with the miners who were washing the grime from their throats. Old Willum's place in the corner was empty as it always was when he was not there, for everyone accepted it was 'Willum's Seat' and no one else used it, not even on a Saturday when the bar was crowded.

Daniel bought himself a pint of beer and pulled a stool over to the corner. The air was heavy with smoke; the ceiling was stained nearly as dark as the old oak beams that supported it, but there was a pleasant deep fire that sent flames licking into the room. Some of the miners and labourers were already in their cups - he could tell by the sudden rise and fall of their voices and by the way that everyone wanted to talk and no one wanted to listen. Larry Collins, whom he had fought as a boy, was at the bar. He had grown into a strong young man with hair as black as the coal he cut and eyes that flashed to the song of his voice.

Daniel was as tall and strong as Larry now but where Larry was dark he was fair, where Larry was loud, he was quiet, and where Larry stood smouldering with unfocussed rage Daniel stood silent and contemplative. They could scarce be more opposite yet their lives were linked by the village and above all by their fight.

Daniel was sitting one quarter to the fire and three quarters to the room which allowed him to watch the happenings at the bar without appearing too inquisitive.

Larry was surrounded by half a dozen of his friends and one of them was saying that his uncle had been at Mafeking. This, he seemed to think, made him an expert on warfare.

The others tried to invade his monologue but the lad kept going against all comers though he converted no one because they all were of one opinion to start with.

At last the miners became bored with the young man and called on him to prove he was such an expert and with that he snatched a broom from across the counter, pulled the dirty bristle to his shoulder and began to bark out an imitation of gunfire.

Larry laughed and took the broom from him. "It only fires blanks," he scoffed. "And from the dust on your shoulder it needs cleaning."

The others laughed and Larry upended the broom and stood it on his shoulder standing to attention as he did. His friends laughed at this and, encouraged, Larry began to march up and down the bar with the broom in his right hand and his left as stiff as a stick. One of the young men brought out a penny whistle and began to play a marching tune. Larry kept time to the music but Daniel noted that the fun had gone out of their faces. At last the tune was finished and the group of young men and all the others at the bar gave a cheer and clapped Larry on his back.

One of the miners ordered Larry a drink saying it had been a fine show.

"It does my heart good to see men of your mettle," he said.

Daniel watched in astonishment as the miners nodded in agreement, full of themselves. "Aye if England needs fighters she's best be calling on us," one of them shouted out and the others called out in agreement.

They were getting even louder in drink now and one of them, Johnny Morrison, raised his glass above his head and said into the silence that his gesture brought: "Aye I can say this. If those Germans are ever so daft as to take us on, every man here will be at the front."

The others clapped and cheered at this and Larry laughed. "Whey man there's nowt in that is there. It will be like taking a chance to see the world." He drank deeply and they all cheered again.

Daniel felt as though the world was a carriage that had left without him, and worse, the truth was he no longer wanted to ride upon it. He had always felt a distance between himself and the other young men in the village but this night, this scene he had just witnessed, distilled it with a clarity that discomforted him.

He had been so preoccupied with the scene that he had

not noticed Old Willum take his seat in the corner. "Young fools!" The old man spat into the fire. "They won't be singing for long when the fighting starts, I can tell you."

Daniel shrugged because what he wanted to say was something so encapsulating, so perceptive, that he could not put it into words. He walked over to the bar to order two pints of beer. Larry came over to him and draped an arm around Daniel's shoulder. The young miner was flooded with good humour. "And here's a lad who'll be with us when the brooms become guns eh Daniel?"

Some of the others went quiet at this for they took Daniel's reserve for weakness, and yet Larry was a respected figure being a noted fighting man.

Daniel smiled anxious to escape this tense little scene. "Get on with you Larry and stop acting daft."

But Larry would not let it rest there. "Aye I'm telling you. This lad here." He patted Daniel on the shoulder. "There's blasting powder beneath this one's quiet surface. And I have good reason to know it." He gave a loud laugh.

"Oh aye," said one of the young miners, thinking that Larry must be joking.

"Oh aye!" Larry repeated the words aggressively. "Danny here bopped me on the nose when we were kids. Aye and at the time he were a lot smaller than me. He fought me at a time when he knew he'd get beat. Not many have the guts to do that."

The others stared at Daniel with new interest. Larry's sudden generosity confused Daniel. It touched his essential innocence that on the one hand there should be this scene which he found repulsive and yet on the other there was this sudden generosity from his former foe.

Neither of them had ever mentioned the fight all those years ago. Indeed they had hardly spoken on the few times they had met, though Larry had always nodded in respect. And now from this little event Daniel felt a confusing bond of comradeship rising in him to a young man who was essentially alien.

He smiled at Larry and patted him on the shoulder. Larry's original suggestion about Daniel and the war had got lost in the subsequent chatter and Daniel used the hiatus to make his escape." I mustn't keep Old Willum waiting for his beer," he said. He clutched the drinks to his chest as he made his way through the crowded room and sat down beside the old man.

"Were they going on a bit?" asked Willum.

Daniel wiped his hand across his forehead. He was beginning to itch with sweat. "They're good lads at heart," he said.

"They're as good as dead if they go on the way they are at present." Old Willum sniffed and spat into the fire.

Daniel was possessed by a sudden thought. "You know what frightens me," he said. "It's just that there must certainly be other groups of lads saying the same sort of things. And a lot of them will be young Germans."

Daniel looked across at Old Willum who spat into the fire again. Daniel saw the wrinkles in his skin, the shrunken shape of the man, the watery eyes and saw him literally as an old man for the first time instead of some catalyst for the past whose mind was so rich with the culture of the countryside that Daniel did not hear the old man complaining of aches and pains. Here was a man whose grandfather had fought at Waterloo, who had had himself been a hero in the Crimea, and who lived his own life at his own pace in his own place.

In a moment of weakness Daniel envied the old man his age and his simplicity. He wished he was far from the pub that night. He wished he was alone in the hills at the start of the day.

"Oh I forgot," he exclaimed. "The lamb's taken."

"Oh aye." Old Willum sucked deeply on his pipe which he had lit with a spill held into the fire. He listened, sucking on his pipe until Daniel had told the tale, and then, because the story of the lamb had inspired memories he began to tell Daniel his own stories; of the reapers working in a great line across the fields with their scythes on harvest days and how the foreman would shout when he saw a race developing between the men and the girls gathering the stacks behind them for he feared he would lose too much of the crop. He told Daniel of the thick slabs of porridge that were brought to the fields to feed the labourers. He told tales from the different seasons, tales of the simple beauty and simple hardship. Daniel sat entranced as the old man in a deep firm voice described the richness and the poverty of it all.

Daniel drank a couple more pints and then rested his

hand on Willum's shoulder. "I must go now Willum. I'll see thee next week."

Old Willum pulled his pocket watch to the fullness of its chain. "It's early yet lad isn't it?"

"Aye." Daniel nodded. "But it's time I went I'm thinking."

The old man understood Daniel's need to be alone though not the reason for it. "Aye lad. I'll see thee next week God willing." He said this every time they parted.

The moon was behind the clouds and the only light in the street came from the windows of the houses and from the open doorways where some of the women stood gossiping.

Some of them called out to him as he passed and he waved in reply. He had got halfway down the street when he heard one of the women hastening up behind him.

He turned and was surprised to recognise Susan Moody for it was rare for the younger girls to stay out on the steps with their mothers.

"What is it, Noisy Boots?" He grinned.

"Nowt at all," she said cheerfully. "I felt like taking the air so I thought I'd walk to the end of the village. That's all."

"Oh," he said surprised. "You'd best not be seen with me or the tongues will be a wagging."

Susan shrugged. "That they'll be already."

They both knew this to be true for courtship was often so clandestine in Milford and the surrounding villages that romances were often kept secret until the engagement was announced. Gossip grew at a rate in such an environment.

"Let them wag if they want," said Susan jerking her head in a little snort. "If I want to take a walk I will do so."

Even in the half light he saw her face stiffen with determination and he found it attractive and amusing in one normally so flippant. They walked in silence for a little way enjoying the warm, still night that was broken only by the occasional burst of laughter from the pub.

Eventually to make conversation she asked:" Are you working Sunday at Mr Meredith's?"

"No." He shook his head.

"What are you going to do then?"

"I'm off to the big city to see my brother."

"Oh."

There was something in her tone that begged a question.

"Why? Why do you ask?"

"Dunno. I just supposed you would be going for a walk in the hills."

He did not reply and she gave a little cough to hide her nerves. "There's folk say that you know a lot about the hills, about animals, about birds and things."

He smiled. "What's a lot?"

"Oh you know. You know what I mean. You see things others don't"

"Well I spend a lot of time up there. Me Mam taught me most of it."

"Aaah." She glanced shyly and slyly at him. "Do you think you could tell me about them sometime? I know nowt really. Nothing special that is."

He hesitated and she added hastily. "I'd only go the once. I know you like it best on your own."

"How do you know that?"

She laughed. "I just do."

He looked at her. Her light brown hair hung loose from a centre parting, her eyes were steady, as black as a mouse's over her white button nose. Her smile was generous and simple. He discovered he liked her.

"You can come a week on Sunday if you wish."

Her face lit with pleasure; she was pleased to have this to look forward to.

"Yes," she said. "That will do nicely. But don't tell a soul mind." She glanced back down the street. "Bloody gossips."

11

"So what do you think?" Harold grinned like a proud parent as he watched Daniel's face open in awe.

"It's so noisy and dirty and busy and huge."

Harold grinned again. "That about sums it up. It took me a month to get used to it."

They were standing in the huge portico of Newcastle Central Station and in the first five minutes Daniel had seen more people than he did in a year in his village. He looked through the spacious entrance to the station as a locomotive gave a huge hiss and moved slowly but with increasing speed from Platform Two. On the broad road in front of him two trams careered past packed with football fans whose raucous cries cut through the general noise of the city.

"Newcastle are playing this afternoon. I think it's a Football Association Cup Tie or some such thing." Harold was enjoying his role as the guide.

Daniel looked west into the city. The enormous, soot-black buildings were stained with droppings from starlings whose cries joined the general cacophony. They walked past the Lit. & Phil. building and turned right, down towards the river. Harold looked upstream "Oh look the Swing Bridge is open there must be some traffic." No sooner had he spoken than a long, thin battleship cut through the flat water. Daniel watched in awe as her three funnels churned smoke into the sombre sky. "What is it?"

"Dunno. Could be bound for Japan. They've been here frequently. Could be one of ours off for sea trial." Daniel turned his attention to other aspects of the river, the tall, dirty buildings that leaned out towards the river, the scuttle of barges taking their loads out to the coal ships, but, above all, the teeming mass of people. Across the road an old woman extolled loudly the value of her stall of second-hand clothes. "Fresh washed. Fresh washed," she bawled. "Nee lice hinnies."

She was competing with the cries of a paper seller who at two-second intervals bellowed "PYEEPER", pausing only when a customer offered him a halfpenny. The shouting match was disrupted as the seller proffered a paper to a man who was wearing a smart dark blue overcoat. An urchin who had been watching the transaction suddenly sprinted forward, his bare feet slapping on the cobblestones. His timing was perfect and as the city gent offered his half penny he flicked up the man's hand, caught the coin and was away. "Yuh little bastard." The paper seller hindered by the pile of papers under his arm, could only call abuse as the boy darted away. The well-dressed customer smiled and offered another half penny.

"Thank eeh kindly sir. It's not the money it's the principle. That's the third time this week."

"Yah dozy bugger," the clothes lady laughed so hard she began to cough. Harold and Daniel walked along the river and back towards the city centre past Sandgate.

The streets were teeming with women in torn shawls and shoeless children who played in the gutters. "They're full of lice," Harold shook his head din disdain.

Sandgate apart, Daniel became aware that Harold was shepherding him towards the more impressive areas of the city. Harold seemed amused by Daniel's open astonishment at the size of the buildings, the width of the great streets, the huge columns of the Theatre Royal and the soaring monument for Grey, the reforming Prime Minister and, amid all the clatter of carts and trams, the hurrying and scurrying of thousands of people. A deafening roar rolled down the hill from the football ground. Daniel almost jumped in alarm. Harold laughed. "It's ok. It means we've scored a goal."

"WE?"

Harold smiled, momentarily embarrassed. "Just an expression," he said. They were walking past St Thomas' Church before he broached the subject that had been on his mind. "I knew they wouldn't come," he blurted the words out unable to disguise his hurt.

Daniel took him head on. "Well if you know that you will know why they didn't come."

Harold laughed harshly. "Well, it wasn't the reason they gave in the letter."

"Your friends come from a different world. Mum was worried there'd be a repeat of the school incident and Dad? Well look at me. You can imagine how he'd look. They said they would come when you were better settled." Daniel sighed for he knew how much their absence must hurt Harold.

Edith and Jud had known too for they refused to meet Daniel's eye when they made their excuses. "It's his friends. What if they…" his mother had hesitated…"don't take to us?"

"Well then they are not his friends." Daniel had immediately regretted the words. They were pompous and pointless for his mother was a woman who thought the Reverend Martin was beyond challenge. He had a sudden vision of her being introduced to Bennett, the atheistic son of a Bishop. She could not have coped.

The seagulls were swirling above them. Daniel glanced across at Harold. They looked an odd pair together, Daniel in his thick grey suit and solid walking boots and Harold in his dark city clothes and black, shiny, thin-soled shoes. Daniel grinned. Then he saw how vulnerable his brother was. He'd pushed the boat out from a tight family in a tight community and was worried that he'd gone too far and had lost them.

Daniel stayed silent because he sensed there was something his brother wanted to say.

"I have never been anything but open about my background and my family." Harold blurted out the words. "Why shouldn't I? For God's sakes you are my family. There wasn't even a decision it just was. And if that invited ridicule well then that person was not worthy enough to be my friend." He paused to take stock of his words. "Aaargh! Why do I always sound so pompous when I talk to you?"

Daniel grinned. "Because you are pompous. In a nice sort of way. If it's any comfort I said roughly the same thing to mum."

Harold stared at him, grateful. "Really!"

They were in a square of large Victorian terraced houses that surrounded a communal garden. "Well here we are. My humble abode." He gestured to one of the houses. It was anything but humble of course. Harold motioned Daniel towards the garden. "The house belongs to Bennett's father.

The Bishop. He believes that Lloyd George is killing off farming and so has moved his money into property." He sat down on one of the high-backed wooden seats that were dotted about the garden. "I sit here often," he said. "I can make believe I'm in the country until some bloody car toots its horn." The garden was ringed with elm trees and round the large flat lawn there were ferns and rhododendron bushes. A Red Admiral danced in the air on its way past them. Harold sat in silence. He had run out of things that he wanted to say and yet he felt he had not said enough.

Daniel punched him lightly on the shoulder. "Come on. Or they'll think you are trying to hide me." They walked to the house. Harold had his own key.

Bennett was sitting at a large kitchen table at the back of the house. He had a shock of black hair, deep eyes and the whitest teeth Daniel had ever seen. He stared into Daniel's eyes as they shook hands. "Harold has spoken so much of you I feel we have met already," he said.

They ate some muffins that Bennett had been toasting and then their host suggested they took a walk so they strolled up the road to a large stone church with a tall steeple. "Grew up among churches I'm afraid. Still I like the green of this one." He gestured to the acre or so of grassland that was ringed with trees. "Harold was saying that your mother made you attend church."

Daniel grinned. "Yes."

"Hmmm. My own question of faith fell at the first hurdle I'm afraid. I watched my father incanting his way down the aisle with all his finery and was consumed by the suspicion that the whole thing was giving him an erection."

Daniel laughed. "We never had such damning proof against religion. Though the Rev Martin's voice was so loud that it made the experience unpleasant."

"Martin?" Bennett picked up the name. "I think he was the chap who got his post after he told one of the gentry that he might be a great artist. If so he has a lot to answer for." Harold and Daniel grinned.

Bennett yawned., "Never felt comfortable with stone and ceremony, you see. It all gives, what do I want to say. It all gives too much the taste of politics."

Harold spoke for the first time. "Our mother has a little place she goes to on her own. It's a little grotto by a stream.

She calls it her holy place. She says she can feel the spirits."

"Hmmm." Bennett considered the holy place. "Sounds a better prospect than my cold churches. At least if you didn't fancy it you could take a picnic."

As they talked Daniel had the feeling that his brother and Bennett were waiting for something or someone. And so it proved. For Bennett with an expert movement flicked out his chain watch from his waistcoat pocket. "La Belle Dom is late," he announced before turning to Daniel with a smile. "She walks this way every day. She says she is a creature of habit though her real reason is so that she can meet Harold on his way home from work."

He waved away Harold's protests. "Methinks the gentleman protests too much!" Daniel grinned at Harold's discomfort and the situation was becoming increasingly anarchic when a call from Dominique brought them to order.

She was wearing a dark bustled dress which she scooped to climb the low railings that ringed the green. "Come and meet my brother." Harold waved to her.

She was exactly as Daniel had imagined her from Harold's description. Tall and upright with deep auburn hair curled in ringlets down to her shoulders which were covered in the dark satin of her dress. Her bottom lip pouted slightly and he sensed her stubbornness. Her grey eyes gazed calmly at him. They were softened by a speckle of freckles over the bridge of her nose. She stared at him with calm assurance as they shook hands. He remembered Harold had said she has half French. He heard her laugh which was as clear as a bell, saw Bennett and Harold dance to her every word, and exaggerate every gesture.

She was not just strangely attractive, she was interesting. He grinned at the way she played with them but to the others his smile had no context. He refused to explain himself to her. "I hope that you have a kind heart," was all he would say. She looked at him quizzically but he sensed she had understood his meaning.

She smiled a slow smile and continued to look at him as Bennett announced that he must continue towards Gosforth for tea with his parents. No one moved and then Dominique said. "Oh well we'll stroll a way with you." She began to walk from the green and they followed her. She linked arms with Daniel and he felt the easy rhythm of her body as they walked. "Brother Daniel." She smiled. "Harold talks of you so much." She stroked his arm. "I like your suit. It's...functional."

"It's the only one I have. There's no call. I work on a farm."

"I know. I know too that you say you intend to live your life as much as possible in what Harold calls the exaggerated feelings of nearness."

"He makes it sound very grand!"

"As far as I can understand it, it sounds very selfish." She fixed him with her large grey eyes. "Sorry to appear so rude but I prefer to speak my mind."

He smiled. "It is obviously selfish."

"And you are comfortable with that."

"People tend to be self-concerned when making decisions about how they are to live their own life."

"Harold worries about you. He says you despise inventions."

"No, though I don't have his enthusiasm for them."

"Inventors change the world more than politicians. How say you?" Bennett's smile was friendly enough though his eyes were piercing.

"Perhaps you are right but politicians still control it. And there have been so many inventions in the last fifty years... I just don't think we can understand them... understand where they are taking us."

"And do you?" Daniel felt the tug on his arm as Dominique demanded his attention.

He shook his head. "No. Though I know it's the end of my little world."

"In what respect?"

"The world is full of coming and going. Eventually it will change my little village."

"And that is bad?"

He shrugged. "I'm as wary of change as the next man. I accept more easily what I am used to. But my way of life, which was my father's way of life, and his father's way of life...well it's ending."

Her large eyes held his again. "How perceptive." She smiled suddenly. "I gather this is your first visit to our city.

It must be quite a shock."

"Yes. I've seen more people today than I do in a year. And it's very noisy compared with what I'm used to."

"And smelly! Do you know how many gallons of water we use to flush away the horse dung from the streets? No of course you don't! Ben will know to the half pint but I don't want to or need to know beyond that is thousands of gallons each day which gives one an idea of the size of the problem." She sniffed at the thought. "Still the advent of the motor car will eventually clear up the pollution."

She noticed he was grinning. "Are you laughing at me and my little campaigns?" She dug him in the ribs with her elbow.

Daniel laughed. "Do you write letters to the local paper? No. I was just thinking how welcome the horse droppings would be at the farms! Perhaps you could export it. There are farms within a couple of miles of the city."

"Aha," said Harold. "You dreamers. To wash it away is a city person's solution to the problem... to give it back to the soil is a country person's solution."

"And never the twain shall meet," said Bennett.

"Precisely," said Harold.

Daniel and Dominique became aware that Harold and Bennett were grinning at them.

"What?" asked Daniel, suddenly flustered.

"Nothing," said Harold. He beamed with pleasure. "It's just the two of you seem to get on so well."

They did. And later, on the train home, Daniel had to admit that for the first time in his life he envied his brother. Dominique was beyond him and the social strata on which he had chosen to live his life. Harold was destined for a life of achievements and she was one of the prizes. His brother was destined to spend his life with a beautiful and fascinating woman and he? At best he would meet someone gentle and homely. The prospect depressed him.

He made the correct noises when his parents pursued him for news. The city was fine; Harold had found a splendid flat and his friends were interesting and able. And Dominique? Her name hung in the air for long enough for him to become aware of the ticking of the large clock by the kitchen window. And what of Dominique? "She is perfect for Harold," he said keeping his voice relaxed and calm.

87

"Just perfect." He resolved in that moment that he would not return to the city.

He did not keep his promise to write to her because he knew she had a power over him and this frightened him.

Instead he threw himself into his work in the hope that in the passing days the memories of her would become less wounding. She never wrote to him and he hoped she had not suffered the wrench of his own experience. He hoped she had viewed him as some quaint chap from the country. And then he remembered how her eyes had deepened at something he had said and he was frightened again. He knew he could have no future with her. She was of Harold's strata. The life Harold would live was a life she could live. And he himself? Daniel knew that he might fascinate her for a day or a week or a month or even a year. Whatever. As their fascination for each other descended into mutual comfort so would their differences become stronger. They were not made to stand the test of time but she and Harold were.

He took no consolation from these thoughts; more a deep sense of hopelessness and doom. Amid all his plans he had never considered that he might fall in love. There was nothing to do but to stay away and to wait for the misery to fade.

12

They met a mile west of the village along the river valley. Susan was wearing the long, black dress she used for work in the fields and Daniel was pleased to note that she had not forsaken her sturdy hobnailed boots.

She had left her big working bonnet in the house and her brown hair was parted, as usual down the middle but pinned carefully down each side of her pale face. She had not thought to bring some food but his own pockets bulged with cheese and onion sandwiches that his mother had made for him that morning.

He was sitting, leaning back against the bend of an alder tree when she came round the curve in the lane. She did not see him at first and her body stooped with disappointment until he gave a little whistle. Her eyes caught him and she walked towards him smiling. "I feared you had thought better of it."

"You've got no food," he said. "Never mind there's enough her for two of us." He patted his pocket. They started along the valley road in silence. Daniel because this was natural to him, and Susan because she felt like a visitor in his home and was anxious not to appear an intruder by breaking his rules.

Their route lay basically in line with the river valley which took them on a slow slope into the hills where the road became no more than a rutted track. He saw the great oak and remembered his walk with Harold.

Susan was gaining in confidence. She pulled a face. "Well Daniel, you've not taught me much yet. Though mind every word has counted."

He laughed at this and pointed to the great oak that stood huge and lonely. "You see that."

"Of course I see it!" she said jibing him again like she did in the fields along with all the other girls.

"Well then, clever boots. Do you know how it came to be

planted there eh?"

She looked at him with a mixture of exasperation and amusement. "Well as it looks at least a million years old. How should I know?"

He shrugged. "It was probably put there by a jay. They bury the nuts to store food and then forget about them often enough."

"Is that a fact?"

He looked at her sharply and saw that she was fascinated so he told her about the oak trees and pointed to the higher land where the forest guarded the horizon. "They're mainly beeches up there. They can stand the dark forest better than the oak in the light soil so they tend to dominate the high land."

Once he started talking like this everything he saw led to him making some observation, a bird, a track mark, or the odd wild plant. By the time they reached the fringe of the forest they were in the full heat of the day. He could see she was tired though she did not complain. He took a small bottle of water from his pocket. "Do you want some now or shall I bury it to get it cool?" he asked. She wiped her forehead dragging some strands of hair from her parting so that they stuck to her damp skin. "Could I have a sip now?" "Just a sip?" He teased her.

"Yes." She looked at him, almost pleading.

"We can sit here for a while," he flopped to the ground. "It's about time we had a bite to eat any road."

He leaned back against a tree and pulled out his sandwiches which he laid on the grass in their wrapping.

She reached out quickly and gnawed into the bread. "All this walking's made me hungry." She was sitting cross legged so that her hobnail boots peeped out from under her long dress.

The ground was hard and dry but they could smell the grass with every gentle waft of wind. Daniel stared at the fields below them with their ribbon of rough stone walls. The trees on the downward slope hid much of the nearside of the valley, but over the river the fields rose up like a canvas.

He wished he was alone because it was as though Susan's conversation kept wakening him from a dream. He chewed moodily on a sandwich as she spoke. "It's funny how hunger increases your like for the taste of food."

"Yes. That's true," he said.

"I've never tasted cheese sandwiches like this before and that's the truth." She chattered on.

Daniel pulled off his jacket and waistcoat and rolled them into a pillow. Susan sensed he wanted solitude or at least silence.

"Am I annoying you?" her pale face turned anxiously to him and he saw her lower lip quiver. He could not escape from her dependence on him; her day was his responsibility.

"No," he said. "It is only that I am used to being on my own and so therefore tend to behave as though I am on my own."

She knew this was only a half truth. She knew her presence was an intrusion.

"I think it best that we had a little nap." Daniel turned his head so that he rested on his outstretched arm. He closed his eyes. He could hear Susan moving about to get herself comfortable. She was more tired than he. He smelled the grass, the heavy scent of it rising sweet and slow in the breeze. Then he began to drift in and out of a light sleep. When he finally woke he was not sure how long he had lain there; he guessed at least an hour.

Susan was still in her dreams. Her thin body lay oddly tangled in her long dress and her arms and legs straggled out like a rag doll. There was no sense of passivity in her shape, more of some internal struggle, yet she lay there soundly asleep. He stared at her and realised that stripped of her impish sense of humour there was a pale plainness about her that he had not seen before. He found this attractive, that the shell that was her body could be so dull, but when that shell was fired up with her vitality she could fizz with humour and life. He was however relieved that she remained asleep for the present so that he could escape into his thoughts. He began to think about his father and his mother and their rows, about his brother and Dominique. What if she had been a village girl...what then? Would Harold still have taken to her?

He knew he was belittling Harold out of jealousy. If Harold had fallen for her that would have been it despite his haughty ways. He was not given to that sort of compromise, career or no career. No, he would have put love first. Had he not insisted that his family come to town? He had, though only after he was confident that he had earned the respect of his colleagues and friends. Daniel sighed. Again he was being unfair to his brother.

It had been a bad time to introduce Susan to the countryside. He needed to be alone so that it could woo him from his feelings for Dominique.

A couple of chaffinches chattered busily in the branches above him. From their marking he saw they were both male. He had seen a whole flock of males last year, tired from their flight from Norway. The females would be further south.

The wind that stirred the trees was damper, colder now; he could feel it in the air and as he looked across the valley he could see storm clouds rolling in. There was nothing they could do. The rain would be on them long before they could get home and he knew from the darkness of the clouds that this would be no shower but teeming drenching rain that would clap them with thunder and chaff their clothes against their skin, heavy, wet, and cold.

Susan too sensed the approach of the storm. She stirred beside him, rolling from her back to her side so that the part of her body that had been warmed by contact with the ground felt the chill of the heavy wind. She sat up suddenly and rubbed her eyes. "It's cold," she said.

Daniel motioned across the valley. "It's going to pour."

She looked at the clouds, not wanting to believe that they were there. "There's nothing we can do," she said at last.

He laughed. "There's always something you can do."

"Like what?" Susan's voice crackled with irritation.

He grinned at her, remembering all the times that Susan and the other girls had gone out of their way to embarrass him. "We'll have to find a tree hollow," he said.

"A what?"

"Somewhere to shield our clothes until the rain goes."

"Eeeh no!" Her voice filled with such alarm that he laughed again.

"Suit yourself but it's either that or getting a right soaking."

He got up and began to walk further into the wood and she followed caught in a flux between rejecting and accepting his proposal.

He did not stop until the sky was hidden by lush green leaves and the trees were at least sixty feet tall.

He turned to her, sure that she had followed. "It won't get much thicker than this and this won't be enough to protect us. A deep roll of thunder seemed to confirm his words. The heavy skies and the translucent leaves gave the air a strange stillness. As he walked from tree to tree seeking cover for his clothes it seemed to her as though he was walking through the velvet air.

The first of the rain was spitting on the green roof before he found what he wanted and he quickly began to undress. He took off his waistcoat and shirt before looking across at Susan who was standing with a finger in her mouth. He smiled. "There's nothing to it. Your dad takes his bath in the backroom when he's home from the pit doesn't he?"

She nodded and the image of her father's white, blue-scarred body slipped into her mind, his muscles knobbly and pale as marble when the coal dust was washed off them. She looked at Daniel. The brown skin of his upper body blended into the gloom so that he and everything around him seemed as one and suddenly she felt no qualms at appearing naked in front of anything so natural. She looked across at him again. He was bending naked before the opening in the tree and she saw that he was as white as her father was from the waist down. Already the rain was boring through the leaves. She took a deep breath and took the pins from her hair so that the locks swung down to hide her body as she began to undress. Once having made the decision she scurried out of her clothes as quick as she could. She did not dare to look at Daniel as she thrust her clothes into the tree. At last she raised herself with her hands clasped over her stomach. She feared he would laugh at her and she thought she would die of shame if some force did not sweep her painlessly away from this scene. She had to summon all her courage to look him in the face. He was pointing at her legs and grinning. Her eyes followed him downwards. Her big black boots were still on her feet shining like two cobblestones. She gave a little giggle and for the first time lost her self consciousness as she bent to take off her shoes. The weight of the rain had bent the leaves but she found the lash of the water strangely warm and exhilarating.

Daniel's skin shone in the rain and the grass which had been so dark before the storm now had a luminous quality. Already the earth was mushy beneath their feet. Daniel started to dance exhilarated by the strange colours that the rain had painted. Even the smooth bark of the beech trees was stained with subtle sheens.

She willed him to come towards her and he did, dancing wildly. She did not move; it was as though they were clothed by the air. Then his arm went round her clutching the back of her thigh as he lifted her and whirled her into the air, pressing her hard into him as he danced to the music in his mind. Their skins were warm and wet as the softness of her body slipped over the hardness of his. She hung over his shoulder watching the world whirl round as Daniel danced. She thought she would faint with desire if this went on; she could hear Daniel's laughter as he dashed in and out of the trees. His laughter, his movements, everything about him filled her with a primitive feeling of release. It was as though they were the only two people in the world at the start of the world. There was nothing; nothing else, just she and he and the forest and the rain. She slipped down his body standing on her toes to kiss him as she reached the ground. She wanted to feel fulfilled as she knew he was fulfilled and this was the only way that she knew. She pulled his head to her with a strength that surprised him.

13

The war came that summer. They were working in one of the big fields when Jack Robson, the postie, gave out the news as he rode over from Swannell with his mail.

"It's war," he shouted, slowing down to a wobble. "It's war. We warned them Germans and now we're going to show 'em."

Only those nearest the hedge could hear him but the news spread like a flame in hay. Some of the girls hugged the men and they started to cheer. Daniel stood like a statue at a carnival. He had long known that the war was inevitable from Harold's letters but now that the moment had arrived he felt numb and apart from all the others though not detached.

Susan hugged him. "Aint it exciting. You know after all this waiting."

"But why?" asked Daniel. "Why?"

One of the men picked up his words. "It's been coming long enough. And now we can get on with it."

"But you're not in the army," Daniel said woodenly.

The others laughed in derision. "We'll get the call soon enough. They're bound to want more men."

By now the few workers who were not in the field had picked up the scent of excitement and they climbed over the hedgerows so that all work came to a stop.

After a while the news reached the village and the church bells began to toll. The situation was so serious that the Rev Martin abandoned his plan for an afternoon's fishing. Instead he stood outside his church as the bell called his congregation to him and he made a long speech about England, her history, her sons, her long line of heroes, and the righteousness of her cause.

Some said it was the longest sermon he had ever preached but no one dared move until he had finished and when at last he called out "God save the King", everyone cheered.

Harold came home six weeks later. There was not a question left in him. He crackled with suppressed energy. Daniel found his brother and his father unbearable. Harold was determined to join up at the first opportunity as were all his friends.

"Mr Ormsby offered me his backing to get a commission but I thought it better to stand on my own feet," he said sternly one night.

Then, on one of his walks, he turned to Daniel as though struck by the thought. "I don't suppose you will be joining up," he said.

Daniel looked down the valley towards the village. "No, I don't suppose I will," he said softly.

Harold stared at him. "You're not a pacifist are you?"

Daniel smiled. Harold did like his categories. "No. It's nothing like that."

Harold shook his head. "Sometimes I think that you do not live in the real world."

"The real world!" Who decides what is real?" Daniel reached out and squeezed Harold's shoulders and stared intently into his brother's face. "You must do as you see fit and allow me to do the same. Be sure of one thing. My world is as real to me as yours is to you."

They turned and began to stroll back to the farmhouse. "Does father give you a rough time?"

Daniel shrugged. "He has a kind heart at the end of it. I think he's frustrated. He never really found his own life to live. I think he fears he could have done more."

Harold's thoughts turned back to the war. "It's so sad," he said. "I was going to suggest that we join up together." He sighed. "But I always knew in my heart I suppose."

Daniel gave him a friendly pat on ther shoulder. "No, it's not to be," he said. He had a sudden vision of himself staring down the lane from his home, sad each time his brother left for the city. He looked about him. The beauty had gone out of the day and there was dampness in the air.

A dozen youths marched stiff and straight, their new suits, their starch collars, their shining boots, their glistening, oiled hair, their stern, fixed, young faces, all emphasising the narrow road between adventure and absurdity.

The whole village turned out to send them off, shouting

and cheering amid tremendous excitement. Only Mrs McQuinn who had brought them into the world shed a quiet tear.

At the head of the column strode Larry Collins and his friends as they marched off towards Swannell. His father was waiting at the station entrance, thumbs jerking into his waistcoat, his flat cap levelled at a jaunty angle, his set smile suggesting that HE was on stage, and that his son was but an extension of himself.

In the furore of the previous evening when all the fathers had got drunk with their sons. Willie Collins had told anyone who would listen that "them Germans" would get a shock when they came up against Larry and his lads.

Someone had straggled some bunting across the station entrance and this rasped angrily in the cold winter wind. The Reverend Martin, though he was beyond his parish, made yet another speech about God and England as the youths stood to attention, stiff as corpses yet full of life, their lips quivering with excitement. Daniel wondered whether the vicar really did believe that God had draped himself in a Union Jack.

The colliery band turned out in full uniform and the train had to wait until they finished their version of God Save the King.

The last note died into the air and the lads scrambled aboard the carriages and hung from the windows as the steam from the train whooshed around them. Old Willum felt his heart go cold. He whispered to Daniel: "They look like ghosts."

Daniel was startled to see Old Willum's eyes wet with tears. "I'm the last one left," he whispered. "The last one left." Daniel knew that he was remembering his comrades from years ago.

Then the train was gone and the fathers and mothers and brothers and sisters broke up into ones and twos as they moved away back to their homes, for there was nothing else for them to do. Some became aware once more of the effects of their drink the previous night.

Daniel had felt a deep despair as he watched the young men leave. It was as though, that by some strange irony, it was his own world that was being invaded. He was sure that the whole thing was madness and that madness was everywhere; that the cause of war had become no more than an excuse to release the aggression that had been building up between industries, between governments, and eventually between peoples.

He had known there was no hope that his world would be left in peace when the travelling tinker added Union Jack flags to his stock that already contained portraits of the King and Lord Kitchener.

The division between he and his father widened the following summer. At first it could be argued that the nation needed all the food it could get and so Daniel's job was as important as any in uniform, but as the crops came in and as his son made no attempt to enlist Jud became increasingly irritated. He liked matters simple so it was easy for him to assume that the war was right and his son was wrong. Added to this the village clearly agreed with him. Indeed there was the odd muttering in the pub, nothing specific about Daniel, but Jud fancied there was a slight coldness between himself and the men whose sons had enlisted.

Worst of all was the feeling that Daniel not only dismissed his father's views but despised them. He felt he had lost his son and this hurt him to the point of resentment.

"Look at what they've done to those Belgiums," he said at one tea time. "Invading them like that and spearing little babies on bayonets."

"Are you sure that is true?"

Daniel's question only enraged Jud the more. "Supposing it is true what are you going to do about it?"

"I don't know."

"You don't know." Jud rapped the table with his fork making his mug of tea shiver. Then his voice softened. "I don't understand you son."

Edith intervened. "Jud don't go on so at the lad." She wiped under Jud's cup before it made a mark. "The lad's confused, anyone can see that."

"He must be the only lad in England that is then that's all I can say."

Daniel allowed his mind to drift away as his parents started on each other.

Daniel felt a detached sort of peace as he looked at his father. He almost felt sorry for him for he sensed that Jud, frequently fearful that his life had been aimless, needed one great gesture to comfort himself. He was too old to be a hero so he lived for that in his sons. That was why he approved of Harold's ambitions and sense of purpose. But Daniel unsettled him with his seeming complacency. To Jud he was allowing life to pass him by, and that was too near to his own failings.

His mother remained neutral during most of these exchanges, only intervening when Jud became too excited. She had no political beliefs, and while she had digested the propaganda that had been thrust at them as easily as most she knew Daniel was much more of a thinking person than she or Jud. Her sons were her life and one in the army was enough.

Harold's first letter as a soldier told them that he and his friends had spent the first few weeks of Army life camped in wooden huts in the grounds of Alnwick Castle.

"It is a beautiful town," he wrote. "So English with its bending streets and to be camped under this magnificent castle...well it seems so symbolic. However our dreams soon came down to earth. The training is mainly drill at the moment, dull and arduous. And as for our proud new uniforms! They arrived within a week but they were navy blue in colour. Somewhat surprised I enquired about their origin and was told they were post office surplus. Of such things our dreams survive!. Nigel (that's Sorrel you know) laughed as much as I did when I told him. He, like me, had marched away very proud and full of a sense of duty or some such thing. We English are too reserved, I think, and so suddenly to be filled with pride for one's country and to be proud of that pride is, well, very thrilling. I feel a bit evangelical!

"Anyway I digress! The mood of the camp is very enthusiastic. We all very much want to get over there and get the job done. Even some of the meaner fellows and there are enough of them, want that and everyone's keenness on this matter creates a very real feeling of comradeship.

"This week we were taken to the moors at Otterburn where we were given shovels and told to dig trenches. I of course with my background was better schooled than most but I noticed a big Irish chap tutoring Nigel on how to dig with a slow easy rhythm which allowed him to put his body weight into each thrust of the shovel. At the end of it Sorrel, who probably had never spoken to a road digger in his life grinned and shook hands with the chap."

The letter went on, pleasant relaxed and chatty, but Jud's deep steady voice filled Daniel with alarm.

The war came at a time when Daniel was at last coming to terms with his life. He was unable to explain it coherently and probably never would but he now felt part of a life that gave him a profound satisfaction. He had dared to stare years ahead, and what he saw did not alarm him. Whereas once he had stood outside from people watching their actions and unable to take part because he had sensed they were false, now he was aware and involved in his own outlets. He was on his own stage, in his own play, at the very time the war demanded he should join the world he had already rejected.

Daniel escaped into the hills at every opportunity. Sometimes he walked the whole day and on others he sat watching the wild life of the countryside until the fading light enveloped him and he merged with the forest. Then one Sunday a solution appeared to him. Before leaving on his walk he picked up a spade, an axe, and a ball of greased string. He followed the meandering road from Milford, up past the Meredith's farm until the road became a track and finally there was nothing. He reached the edge of the forest that stretched high and dark up into the hills. He strode into the forest for six hundred paces until the giant beeches rose one hundred feet or more in their fight for light.

He selected a tree and moved cautiously upwards until he came to a branch that was about three inches in diameter at its apex to the trunk. His axe, which he had sharpened and oiled the previous night, made short work of cutting it free.

For an hour the forest rang to the sound of axe on wood until at last he stood over a pile of timber steaming in his own sweat. He began by tying two of the smaller branches into two sides of a triangle. He repeated the process four times and then used three, longer struts to support the apex and the extremities. He stepped back to view his work. The structure which stood about four feet high and eight feet long resembled the skeleton for a primitive roof. He completed the work by tying some shorter pieces of wood in a cross lattice to the frame. That afternoon he cut long strips of turf to cover his roof. Finally he brought some round, heavy stones up from the river bank to secure the base.

Daniel left his shelter for a week and when he returned he found some overnight rain had seeped through the turf and into his shelter. He spent the morning cutting large strips of bark from the beech trees. He laid these between the turf and the latticing. He had a primitive home and, luxury of luxury, enough space to sit inside.

He was eighteen years old that spring and there was not a man in the county who was better equipped to live in a forest.

He knew his trees; how to used hard wood on soft wood to make a flame; he knew the birds and where they slept; he knew the fungi from the beefsteak that grew on oaks to the giant puffballs that were found in woods and grassy places; he knew the plants and their fruits and roots; he knew you could eat the young leaves of the primrose, and that you could create a coffee tasting drink from dandelion roots. He knew rabbits often burrowed near elder bushes at the edge of the forest. He knew too that rabbits were creatures of habit so were much easier to catch than hares. He knew he could survive here until the winter at least and then… he shrugged his shoulders at the thought. Time would tell. This was his own battle for survival and he suspected he was better equipped and prepared than Harold was for his.

He worked steadily in the fields for the rest of the week and on the Friday took the afternoon train into Alnwick. The market town was teeming with soldiers and he could see the huge camp of huts in the grounds of the castle. He thought fleetingly of trying to contact Harold but knew it would be a futile gesture in the crowded camp.

Instead he toured the shops buying a large rucksack into which he put pans, plates, cutlery and as many tins of food as he could carry. His rucksack was bulging as he made his way up to the station. There was no sign of rain so he left the rucksack overnight under a hedge that skirted the far field of his father's holding

He rose first the next day, picked up the sandwiches he had made the night before, collected his rucksack and was gone before anyone had risen. The dew was still on the grass and the early birds were stamping on the turf to entice the worms. He struggled up the hill and by the time he had reached his shelter his shoulders were sore with the straps and his back and legs were aching. By now he realised that his life in the forest would take him over a large area which meant that he would need a number of temporary shelters. The simplest took the form of a snapped off branch which he secured to a bough of the tree. On another day he came across a large beech tree which had crashed to the ground. He used the trunk as a wind break and built a sloping roof using a lattice of wood to support strips of turf.

On the higher land he built a two sided wind break in the form of a primitive fence that cut into the slope. He protected this with a ditch to divert any running water and covered it with branches he chopped from a tree.

He travelled to Alnwick every week now to buy food and utensils. On one trip he bought a dozen large canvas sheets from a pawn shop.

He planned to dig a large food store near his shelter and to cover the sides and base with wood but when he arrived at the site he discovered that a freak overnight frost had made the ground impossibly hard so he busied himself cutting four, foot-long lengths of wood. He walked over to the rabbit warren and scouted for their trails. The ground was still rock hard so there were no fresh prints but Daniel knew that rabbits not only ran along the same paths time and again but also ran in the same footsteps.

He used a knife on the ground to set up a couple of traps with steel wire nooses. He tested the sticks for purchase and walked back to the shelter.

When he returned to the warren a couple of hours later it was as he hoped; a rabbit lay wild-eyed and half-choked with the noose tight around its neck. It made one frantic attempt at escape as Daniel approached and its paws threatened to tear his skin as he took hold of its ears and with one quick flick of his wrist he snapped its neck.

The following week he dug the hole, hammered the wood in round the sides and put a further layer at the base which he covered with bark to insulate all his tins from the ground. He covered the hole with some more struts of wood, covered them with a cut of canvas and placed the original turf on top of this. He was ready to go and this knowledge acted like a buffer in his mind to the assaults of his father who daily grew more surly at the refusal of his son to join up as more and more of the young men of the village answered Kitchener's call for volunteers.

Throughout the winter Daniel prepared himself to face any eventuality. He knew where the pheasants slept, knew that his main shelter was seven hundred paces from the nearest stream, which, although shallow, was cool and clear.

He bought himself a large old stewing pot which he estimated could hold a week's supply of water and then dug a hole similar to the one he had prepared for his food. He took the largest of his pans to the stream and used it to fill a bucket. The stream was only a couple of inches deep and he found he was disturbing the sediment so each time he dipped the pan into the water he moved slightly upstream. It took him ten trips to fill the stewing pot.

He covered the pot with a strip of canvas which he secured with string. When he returned a week later he was relieved to discover that the water was still fresh. Even so he decided that every drop would have to be boiled. He spent two days touring his domain and was pleased to note that the potatoes and swede he had planted in random patches of fertile land had grown undisturbed and unnoticed.

At last there was nothing more to do and he felt the deepest sense of elation in months. He had been depressed at the prospect of being forced to fight in the war. He felt he had won himself back from the madness of the world and the struggle that lay ahead was one which he could relate to and therefore respect. He told himself that at least his fight was for himself and not for, and at the command of, outsiders.

Before he left home in the spring he wrote a note to his mother and father trying to explain his actions. He paused frequently as he struggled to find the right words.

"Dear Mum and Dad,

"I'm going away for a while because I am not going to fight for something that doesn't concern me.

I promise that if the Germans invade Milford I will come back to fight. Indeed if they threaten Milford by invading this country I will fight that too. "For the rest of it I just don't feel anything.

Your loving son,
Daniel"

He knew his words were inadequate even to himself never mind to his parents whose minds would already be clouded with their own preconceived feelings and prejudices. He knew that little of what he wanted to tell them would reach them but he had to try.

It was warm that first night and he left the ends of his shelter open to improve the ventilation. He awoke felling slightly stiff but the earth smelt good. He was glad to be alone.

14

Edith blamed Jud for Daniel's departure because there was no one else for her to accuse.

"I hope you're satisfied now!" Her voice cracked like a whip and in those few words she invested all her frustrations all her disappointments and all her fears. Jud had his uses!

The look in her eyes was one of disgust, almost hatred. It took Jud by surprise so that he could only stammer "I only had my say. The lad'll see sense and he'll be back." They were only words, he knew, scattered out while he collected his thoughts.

She seized on them.

"If you think that you don't know your own son."

He said nothing because he could not think of anything to say, but Edith was not finished with him yet. "Has it ever crossed your mind that he has done what he has done and said what he has said because he is strong, not because he is weak." She began to sob. Jud retreated to his work. At the door, he said:" You do me wrong Edith if you do not think I love the lad."

It took a week for news of Daniel's departure to reach the village. Mr Meredith had assumed that Daniel was absent from work because he was ill.

Eventually he walked across to the little cottage and Jud told him "He's gone away." Jud spoke in such cold fashion that Mr Meredith did not ask where. Two weeks later one of the shepherds mentioned that he had seen a fair-haired lad striding towards the hills early one morning. Susan and some of the other girls knew of his love of the country and through a process of repetition their conjecture that he had 'gone to live in the wild', became a certainty as the days passed.

There was no immediate sense of outrage. If anything his departure was lost in the general excitement. None of the men from the village had as yet gone to the front and their letters home had one common theme: they were all fed up with the training and they could not wait to get into action. Only Old Willum remembered the bravado of his own letters sixty years ago when he had been off to fight the Russians. But he said nothing. It was still a great adventure to the rest of the villagers; there was no thought of failure or death, hence there was no sense of disgust at Daniel.

When one of the more bitter women pointed out his absence while others were serving their country Mrs McGrath folded her arms emphatically and said in a voice that would brook no interruption: "I've brought the whole lot into this world. Every young man and every young lass too, and I'll tell you one thing I knows and that is that yon Daniel is blessed by God. He hasn't got an evil thought in his head.

" I don't know why he's a doing what he's doing but I do know that nothing bad is the cause of it because there's no bad in the lad. So there."

It was the longest speech she had ever made and the most effective. None of the women dared to argue with so great an authority as Mrs McGrath. They kept their opinions out of her hearing.

Indeed there were some women who supported Mrs McGrath. They recalled Daniel's cheerful rejoinders to them as they stood on the doorsteps of an evening; how he had always smiled as though it was coming from inside, a smile that lit up his fine looks that could warm a woman's memories on a winter's night. The war too seemed more distant in the village. The initial excitement had gone and not one of their sons had fired a shot at the Germans.

The mood which Edith faced when she walked into the village to buy a new pan was reserved, not because of any deep animosity (which she had been expecting) but because she and the village women were conscious of an embarrassing difference between them. If she or they had said something to bridge the subject on that first day it might have ended then. However as time went on it became more difficult to break the silence and Edith began to find a resolve from it and she became more determined to defend her son. Jud felt the difference as keenly as did Edith though for a different reason. He was a modest man at heart, though he was confident that given the chance he would have excelled in war. He would have been an outstanding soldier rather than an ordinary one and he could not understand Daniel's reluctance to become involved given the certain righteousness of the cause. He knew his son was a brave as anyone for he had seen him in a number of situations. In particular he remembered the day one of the farm girls had got between a cow and its calf and Daniel had been first to see the danger. He'd charged his shoulder into the beast's flank distracting it until the girl had scampered clear. However, notwithstanding Edith's anger and his love for his son, his own pride was hurt that Daniel had not answered Kitchener's call and in his weaker moments he allowed himself to feel guilty.

The men still talked to him when they met in the lanes but the subject of Daniel was never broached though Jud knew they must talk about his son in his absence. He felt an increasing gap between himself and the villagers.

It was with pride then that Jud learned from Harold that he had been sent to France.

He was the first son of the village to go out and that gave Jud something to grasp.

Harold's letters were not as regular now and sometimes two or even three arrived on the same day. Jud no longer read the letters out loud. There seemed no point now that there was just the two of them. Besides Edith could not be expected to leave the envelopes unopened while he was away in the fields when their son was in France and possibly in danger.

Harold's letters retained their chatty tone but as the weeks passed Edith noticed a subtle change. It was not anything that she could specifically identify and Jud put it down to "a mother's worries." But week by week Edith became more certain that Jud was blinded by pride of his son and that Harold was holding something from them.

He mentioned that he was going to the front but nothing more. There was none of the observations or comments that he delighted in when describing his other experiences. Instead he spoke of 'a job that had to be done', told them that 'the men were in good spirits and were confident of victory', even though 'the Germans were fighting men'.

That last phrase wriggled in and out of Edith's consciousness as though it had a life of its own. It came to her each time she learned of the casualties as the war became bogged down in the trenches.

Jud was so cheered by Harold's involvement that he took to going to the George once more. In his simple way this development allowed him to put Daniel to the back of his mind but events were not to allow his son to remain there.

Willie Collins had hit a bad patch in the seam that week. He had hacked away until it was only temper that kept him going. Each evening he went straight from work to the George and sat glowering and brooding all night. His body and neck had thickened with age. He had lost the supple movement of his youth and his belly seeped over his broad black leather belt. But where speed had gone there was weight and beneath the fat he was still thick with muscle. There was not a man in the pit who would stand against him young or old when he was in an evil mood so there was a hush at the bar when Jud walked in an ordered a pint.

Jud nodded to the room in general and walked across to the window near Old Willum's empty seat.

Willie ordered another drink and began to stare at Jud. He had narrow, dark eyes and a mean, thin mouth and this together with his short neck and thick shoulders had frozen many a man before a blow was struck. He had been seeking trouble to release his anger all week, and though he had seen Jud a number of times since Daniel had disappeared and done nothing, tonight the sight of the farmer sitting there set him smouldering.

There was no one near him when he began talking. At first his voice was merely a mumble and then his tone grew deeper. Those near him stopped talking for fear that he might pick on them.

"My lad's going over next week." He stared round the room not finding a pair of eyes that would meet his own. Jud was looking out the window up the slope of the far valley, noting that one of the farmers, Mr Marsden, looked set to have a healthy wheat crop in a big field that had lain fallow the previous year. He began to hear the silence and he turned from the window to find Willie staring at him.

"I said my lad's going over to France next week Jud."

Jud nodded. "Aye. Harold's been over there a while."

"Oh," said Willie. "I thought he was out skulking in them there hills,"

There had never been a louder silence in the George. Len Harking froze in horror. He even forgot to look for his stick. Jud might have been slow to pick up the atmosphere but he made up for lost time after that. He never said another word. He just rose quickly and smoothly in such a way that some remarked later that he was like Daniel in his movements.

Willie jumped to his feet as Jud advanced and threw a punch but the farmer turned his hips and the blow bounced off the muscles of his left shoulder. But Jud's movement had not been to avoid the blow but to strike one himself. Consequently he lost neither momentum nor balance. His hips twisted as his right fist struck forward like a piston and his breath exploded through his nostrils .His body rose to balance on the balls of his toes so that when his knuckles struck the side of Willie's jaw there was not an ounce of Jud's body that was not behind the blow. Willie span back and fell to the floor. One of his flailing arms struck a glass from the bar and his head hit the stool on which he had been sitting seconds before. Willie Collins felt the impact of neither. He was already unconscious. Jud stood over him for a second, willing him to get up because his anger had not abated. But Willie did not move.

Jud leaned over and felt his chest and someone broke the silence at last. "My God Jud! Have you killed him?"

"His head's too thick for that," Jud said forcefully. He looked about the room. "It'd be a brave man to call my son to me again. Goodnight gentlemen." And with that he strode to the door leaving his beer unfinished for the first time. When Willie regained consciousness and was helped to his home they looked at the glass that Jud had left and spoke in awe of the blow that had felled the hardest man at the colliery. There were some who remembered that Jud had beaten Willie at arm wrestling years ago but always the conversation returned to the mighty punch and every man said that they had seen nothing like it and that it would have killed a lesser man than Willie Collins. One of the miners, Joe Thirkell said: "I don't think that Willie was ready." But the others just looked at Joe because it was well known the he could start an argument in an empty house. The truth was that they all delighted in the fight because they were all great tale tellers for that was how the news was passed in those days. They knew they had been lucky enough to see one of the great events of the village and most of them were delighted at Willie's humiliation anyway.

For a long time the fight was a greater event than news from the war for it had happened here in their midst and the men could sit outside on their haunches of an evening and whenever the conversation lulled there was always someone who chuckled and asked: "Do you remember the time Jud Lawson felled Willie Collins with just one punch?" And of course they all did but it did not stop them retelling the tale and reliving it once more. Indeed, as time went on it became apparent that there was hardly a man for five miles who had not been in the pub at the time and Lennie Harkin once remarked with a smile that that if everyone who had seen the fight had been at the fight he could have retired on the night's takings.

But if Jud was the hero of the moment it was only in the eyes of others. To Jud, Willie's remark was proof of what he had always feared... that the villagers would never forget Daniel's sortie into the wilds.

His head hung heavy as he sat at the kitchen table that night and told Edith of all that had happened in clear and simple terms that gave his story a dignity that Edith thought was beautiful.

"I don't back the lad in what he has done," he said at last. "But he is my son and there's no call for what Willie said is there."

Edith looked at him for a long time as he stared at the table. As he told his story she was aware of a decisiveness and purpose about him that was lacking so much of the rest of his life. She saw the sleeping hero in him and it thrilled her greatly. In that moment she realised that for years now she had seen only his weaknesses and none of his strengths. It was as though a great depression lifted from her. She rose from her chair by the fire and crossed the room to lay her hands gently on his shoulders. His jacket was cool from the night air. She cradled his head to her breasts and stroked his brow.

"You did right Jud," she spoke softly.

Jud nodded his head. "He's our son," he said.

The light was above him casting a shadow down his face

but catching the strong brow nose and chin. She saw in him a nobility that surprised her. She kissed his mouth with a tenderness that startled them both.

They were united by circumstance now. Edith rarely went to the village and Jud worked long hours in the fields, At night he found odd jobs as he had done in the old days. He could not bring himself to return to the King George. Ironically most men in the village had hoped that he would do just that because the feeling about Daniel was far outweighed by the desire to see the hero of the hour.

Old Willum made the most of the fight each night that he sat in his special chair. He had long learned that longevity carried with it the privilege of being allowed to speak candidly about anything that moved him. "And you think that such a man could be the father of a coward?" he asked. "I tell you don't understand nothing."

Joe Thirkell pressed him. "Well why did the lad do it?"

Old Willum just laughed and said: "You must work that out for yourself."

The truth was that he was not sure himself though he bitterly regretted Daniel's disappearance for he had recognised a spirit of life in him that was more vibrant than anyone he had ever met.

15

The train was crowded on Harold's first leave and he stood in the aisle of his rocking carriage using the company of his fellow soldiers to hold back the phantoms. But the memories would not be denied; they hid then drifted back into his conscious, finding him out like a nightmare in sleep.

It was better, he decided, to be at the front for at least there his fears were physical and therefore, to some degree, disposable. He found himself talking incessantly to strangers on the train. Some of the soldiers asked him where he had been. Only the rookies wanted to know what he had done and he saw himself of six months ago in their eager faces. He could have told them he had come from another world but they would not have understood.

He saw the postman at the station and remembered his first uniform. Then he remembered the courage of Sorrel, the death of Selby and Bennett and he remembered opening the trench coat of Smyth-Woodford and seeing his belly sprawl out like a barrel load of worms.

In the beginning there was nothing more shocking than the language of the men which was the foulest he had ever heard.

The drilling in the training camp was incessant. Most of the instructors were Boer War veterans who thought the Empire had been built on the bayonet. Some days they were taken to the moors at Otterburn where they dug long, zig zag trenches.

Most of his comrades thought no further than their next visit to the local whore or the next time they could drink themselves into oblivion. He had never realised how bleak their lives were. Some of them though excelled at the football and boxing competitions that were organised in the grounds of the great castle. He was glad that like him Sorrel, Selby, and Bennett had refused the opportunity to become officers. The four of them spent most of their spare time on long walks along the river or into the hills. He surprised them with his countryman's knowledge as he pointed out birds and trees and attached little bits of history. "I confess much of it comes through listening to my brother," he told them with a laugh. For the remainder he sent letters to home and to Dominique. When he wrote to her he felt released from constraints of the past and his tone was frank and tender. In this he had been helped by Bennett in his abrupt fashion. Harold had spoken to him of "the strange nobility of war". Bennett stared hard at him as he progressed with his theory. "It seems to me that to believe in something so deeply that one is wiling to give one's life for it gives that life a deeper meaning." He became aware that Bennett was grinning.

"Don't be such a pompous ass," said his friend. "I hope you're not writing such rubbish to Dom. You'll frighten the life out of her."

Out on the moors the men used flares to synchronise their advance with the non existent artillery that, they were told, would in reality be using a new tactic called creeping barrages.

The rifle instructors were obsessed that every man should be able to fire his Lee Enfield at twelve rounds a minute. When one of the men plucked up the courage to ask why his sergeant stiffened and said sharply: "Because son when the Hun comes at you the faster you can fire the better. Trust me."

At their final target practice a rumour went round that they would be dismissed if they did not pass. One of the men, Dalby, a small Glaswegian, who had moved to Newcastle in search of work and who had only joined up after a drinking session, confided to Harold that he was going to miss the target deliberately. Dalby used Harold as a confessor. He was always showing off to him like a dog with tricks, always over reacting, always complaining the loudest, always wanting to be noticed.

As soon as he fired his last shot Dalby stepped down from the butts and gave Harold a broad wink. But when his scorecard came back his narrow, freckled face opened in amazement. Someone had pierced his target card with a pencil to record a perfect score.

Dalby shook his head. "The bastard! The bastard! And him as is meant to be a gentleman an' all."

Two weeks after the target shoot they were in France, sea sick from a rough crossing, exhausted and stiff from long rides on trains and cattle trucks. They had been scheduled to practise manoeuvres at one of the big camps to the west of the lines but the Germans mounted a big push the day before their arrival so they were hurried up to the front.

They were billeted in a village two miles from the lines. The whitewashed walls were stained with thick layers of dust stirred up by troops and traffic. The villagers had all moved out a lifetime ago. Many of them had left their possessions. The straw mattresses were alive with lice.

Harold was lucky. He billeted in a cottage at the far side of the village and slept in a bunk bed usually reserved for officers. They could hear the gunfire and the scream of shells, but nothing landed near them and after a few days they ignored the sounds.

Within a week they were moved up through the support trenches. Harold could not but help stand on a fire step to take a quick look out across no man's land despite the obvious contempt of some of the veterans. One of them spat. "Just put a fucking bull's eye on your head." He spat again. "Daft fucker!"

Another, friendlier veteran grinned. "It's sniper time."

The snipers controlled their lives, he discovered. They shot at anything that moved, not just in the front lines but in the support and reserve trenches. Their latest victim had died bringing up the cans of supplies to the front line. The previous week a man nicknamed Short Arse Watkins had joked that he was safer than most on account of him being so small. An hour later he was dead. The sniper himself had been captured the following day. He was shot out of hand and left lying in a shell hole.

Harold was astonished by the desolation in no man's land. There was not a blade of grass left. All had been blasted away and the brown dark earth was gouged with shell holes. In a few of them blood-red poppies grew defiantly amidst the carnage. He saw the barbed wired protecting the German lines about eight hundred yards away straggling along the higher land, always on the higher land. To his right, roughly midway between the lines there stood the stump of a tree.

What it had been he could not guess but it was about five feet high without a leaf or a branch left attached to the trunk, which stood out like jagged teeth at the top. Harold's platoon was told to follow a trench line and this zig zagged south until they picked up a support line and then another until they struggled up a slope towards a small wood. Sorrel looked white and ill. "My God did you smell those latrines?" He gasped. They all had.

The German 5.9s opened up almost as soon as they arrived and they all raced for cover. It was always the same: one short, one long, and then all hell if you were in the target area.

One of the veterans tried to pretend that his dug out was full but Harold snarled at him and pushed him to the ground so that he and Sorrel were inside before the man could protest further. There were about half a dozen other men in the shelter. Harold stared at the roof supports, a line of tree trunks. One of the veterans grinned. "Don't worry son. The fuckers are tougher than the wife's corsets." Harold smiled back, glad of at least an attempt to welcome him. He was no longer conscious of the swearing.

The barrage was aimed at the British guns to the west of the wood. It ended after half an hour and Harold clambered out into the open feeling a real soldier, possessed by a strange sense of elation, as though he had passed some sort of test.

A large food urn arrived in a small cart pulled by a donkey in the late afternoon. He hadn't eaten since breakfast and he devoured the basic fare of bully beef and beans. He could smell the grass, sparse though it was in the wood and feel the shade of the trees. He felt more at home here than in the trenches though he would not admit it to anyone.

After they had eaten, Robertson, their sergeant, made them dig latrines. "Can't have you shitting on the daisies can we?" His handsome face lit in a huge grin.

Harold awoke shivering in the dew. In the warmth of the evening and amidst all the excitement he had forgotten to lay out a groundsheet. They were given warm tea and rough biscuits for breakfast and then ordered down from the wood to do repair work on one of the roads. Lieutenant Smyth-Woodford strolled ahead of them.

He rarely spoke directly to Harold or any of the men,

preferring to communicate through Sergeant Robertson who he always addressed as "Sergeant" in the low casual drawl that pervaded most of his speech.

He had steady, light-blue eyes, but his downy moustache only emphasised the youth that he was trying to hide. Harold judged him to be about 20 and the product of his public school corps.

Sergeant Robertson viewed him as an amateur, possibly a dangerous one with his affectations. The Sergeant obeyed him instantly but Harold detected a tempered exasperation at some of the commands and he suspected that Robertson would find some way of avoiding some of the orders if he believed they were likely to bring disaster.

There were dark rumours that some incompetent officers had been shot by their own men during attacks. Harold refused to believe this could be true but then one day he caught Dalby staring at Smyth Woodford with a lean and hungry look. His narrow eyes met Harold's and Dalby muttered: "Fucking hero hunter. He'll get us all killed."

They marched briskly in single file out of the woods. The pale spring sun was peeping hesitantly like a stranger from behind the clouds and the air was warm. They could see nothing of the front line or the support trenches as they moved in a rough south west direction through the wood and along a dirt track which led to a lane.

He recalled the walk from his home down to the village at Milford. They reached the road within half an hour. The 5.9s had got its range and pitted it with half a dozen huge holes.

They were set to work filling them with earth Dalby began to curse the heat as he shovelled the dirt up from the side of the road so that Harold could scoop it into the holes. One of the other soldiers, Rogers, blinked myopically at this tirade of cursing. "The sooner we get this filled in the sooner the ambulances can get up and down with the injured," he said in his peculiar Midlands monotone.

His views were not welcome to Dalby who began a new bout of cursing which called into question the existence of Rogers' parents. Harold looked at the limp, gangling Rogers and the incandescent Dalby. Only the army could have thrown together two such unlikely companions.

Before Dalby could launch some new assault the

Germans opened up with their guns again. This time they were using whiz bangs, hoping that the shrapnel would catch the workers on the road. Smyth-Woodward strolled up and down his unit's stretch of the lane whistling softly. He held his leather gloves behind his back tapping them gently against his tunic and with his puffed out trousers and gleaming leather boots he had all the airs of a man waiting for his groom to provide him with a horse.

Get into the ditch, you men," he shouted, and then, as the soldiers scrambled for cover he strolled away as though he was walking round a cricket ground.

Dalby looked at the retreating figure. "The crazy fucker!" He shook his head. Then, to lend weight to his words the stretcher bearers began to jog past. Two of them stopped near Harold and rolled their limp burden into the side of the road. Their eyes met Harold's stare. "We'll cart him away later," said the larger of the two men. "Can't help him any more." He had a sing song Welsh accent that sounded ridiculously cheerful given the circumstances.

Harold was held by the stare of the dead man. There was no mark that he could see but his face was white. He had steeled himself that he was bound to face such incidents but the suddenness of the confrontation had got past his defences and he uttered an involuntary whimper. He recovered quickly but too late to escape the notice of the veterans. "OK. So long as he doesn't get in our way," he said.

The ambulances could not reach the wounded because of the state of the road and the line of stretcher bearers became longer and more urgent. The whiz bangs were still bursting over them forcing the bearers to keep to the ditch which thankfully was about five foot deep. After an hour the firing stopped and the queue of injured and their helpers, thinned and then disappeared. Harold and his comrades were ordered back on to the road.

That evening they marched back to the woods. Harold found himself between the lugubrious Rogers and the inflammatory Dalby.

"It's tradition you know," Rogers spoke for the first time as they broke ranks on the fringe of the wood.

"Eh!" Dalby could make even "Eh" sound aggressive.

"The officers not scrambling for cover. It's tradition."

"Bollocks. It's just that little public school twat putting on a show." Dalby glared. "The Germans should have given me a mortar. I'd have got the bastard."

Rogers continued as though he had not heard Dalby. "I read it," he said his voice strengthening with certainty. "At Trafalgar none of the officers were allowed to duck. The men hit the deck but the officers remained standing." Rogers' nasal Midlands's accent was suddenly transformed into startlingly realistic Standard English. "Bad form to show fear to the enemy, don't you know."

Dalby stared at Rogers with the expression of a man who had just heard a corpse speak. "Bollocks," he said at last when he had recovered himself.

Rogers shrugged and walked towards the smell of food. Some soup, thin stew, and tea had been brought up from the kitchens.

They were assigned to digging duty for the rest of that week. There was some more shelling every day but none near enough to their section to cause alarm. Only Rogers was depressed by this. "Oi've been thinking, Harold."

Harold looked up from his shovel "Yes?"

"It's just our bit of road may be alright but what about the other buggers? Down the road like." He had decided to give Harold the benefit of the full extent of his thoughts. "Supposing our stretch is ok but there's holes in front and behind. What the fuck eh?"

Harold shrugged his shoulders. "We can only make sure our bit is ok. It's the same for everybody."

They became used to the trail of dead and wounded. Smyth-Woodward continued his stroll around as if he was out in the park. Dalby just looked at him and shook his head eloquently.

On the fourth day Harold was working in a ditch as Smyth Woodward came across another officer from his old school. They stood in the lane, both slim and elegant asking about mutual friends.

"I met D'Arcy last week." The other officer had a slightly deeper voice but the same slow casual air. "You know D'Arcy of Upper House."

"God yes! Of course I knew him. Mad as a March hare."

"Well he's not changed," the officer gave a laugh. "Do you know he was prospecting about riding his hounds at their lines?"

They both shook their heads and laughed. "He thought it a good idea except he wasn't sure whether the dogs would attack the Germans."

Below them Harold and Rogers worked with their shovels. Rogers had learned to copy the easy unhurried rhythm of Harold's digging. They caught each other's eye from time time but neither spoke. Harold did not dare to even glance at Dalby.

Smyth-Woodford swatted his shin high boots with his riding crop. "Bloody boring this, don't you think?"

The other man shrugged. "Got to be done Algie."

"Yes," Smyth-Woodford protested. But it makes one feel like a foreman for a bunch of navvies."

The other officer laughed. "I expect it will hot up soon."

Smyth-Woodford shook his head. "We haven't even fired a shot yet. Bertie."

"Aaah. I have you there."

"You mean you've been up there already." Smyth-Woodford couldn't keep the boyish curiosity out of his voice.

"Oh yes. For a month as near as dammit. Been over the top once."

"Gosh!" Smyth-Woodford's veneer of authority was replaced by boyish wonder now. They walked down the lane.

"Oi was in service at one of the great houses once."

Harold turned to look into Roger's white, earnest face.

"They were just like those two fuckers. They held conversations in front of you as though you didn't exist." He grinned. "You and your brave new world eh. You've got a long way to go Harry boy." With that he launched his long-limbed frame up on to the road where he had been slinging his muck. "I feel like a fucking foreman for a bunch of navvies." Again Rogers's skill as a mimic startled Harold. He stared at the retreating figure, troubled by one question. How had Rogers come to read about the officers at Trafalgar?

Harold was the only soldier to get off the train at Swannell station. The engine chugged away into a tunnel and was gone. He watched the passengers drift away and then stood listening to the birds chirping. As he walked the long road up the valley there was a battle going on in his mind and he was trying to make Dominique win it over Smyth-Woodford. He looked at his hands; they were large and empty but the night before they had held her body. She had whispered in the dark and her hair was damp with the heat of her lovemaking. She was naked; she had shed her clothes and with them the person who lived within the strictures of polite society and conventions was gone too; she now answered a more primitive call. They had made love again and then he had told her that he must dress to catch the train home.

She had said that he should hide like Daniel and that she would hide with him but they had both known they did not have that type of courage; that they needed to live within not without. Even the suggestion had shocked him for he knew she was willing to give up everything for him, even her position in society which was the very thing she had been trained for and the very thing to which he aspired. She cared little for it and valued it less beyond her family and friends. She told him that mannered society anaesthetised her sense of life. They'd been walking to the station and they passed an urchin selling flowers in the huge portico. "Come the winter," he said. "That girl will still have no shoes."

Dominique had blinked at him not knowing what to say, until on impulse she ran to the girl and pressed a sovereign into her hand.

He remembered the words of Bennett who had told him: "I wonder whether I will ever escape my wealth and you your poverty."

"Escape?"

Bennett had smiled, "Into something pure. Like your brother."

Another conversation came into his mind.

He had told Dominique that he had always feared that she would prefer the rebellious Bennett to himself.

She had laughed a deep ragged laugh.

"No Harold. You will be the reformer not Bennett for it is not in your nature to ignore injustice. Bennett will rejoin the establishment once he was worked out the God thing and his father." She smiled at him. "I always knew that. But that was not what attracted me to you."

"What was it?"

She shrugged her slim shoulders. Why analyse it. I just felt this instant attraction."

In the hedgerows the grass seeds had grown, wispy and yellow; he recalled Smyth-Woodford's moustache.

"Funny thing vanity." Once more Harold was being assaulted by Rogers' rolling vowels.

"Really."

"Well look at him and that moustache."

"Must I?" He glanced down the trench at the officer who was shaving carefully in a broken mirror.

Rogers continued as though he had not been interrupted. "The world looks at the pathetic bum floss and sees a boy trying to be a man. But what does he see eh? He sees proof of the man he wants to be."

Perhaps it would be better if he had dark hair," said Harold.

"But he hasn't." Rogers grinned.

Smyth-Woodford's moustache showed even in the hooded light of the torch as they crouched, waiting in the trench. He was reading his orders for the tenth time and the light also caught Sorrel's face which was stiff with nerves. Some of the shells had uncovered the bodies of men killed in a previous attack and the heavy stench hung in the damp night air. Harold could hear someone retching and he tied a handkerchief over his face but the deep stink still got through to turn his stomach. There were new frontiers every day. The first lice, the first stench of death, the first dead man, and now, the first attack.

The first wave moved off at 3 am. Harold watched them climbing the ladders, heard them advancing cautiously through the wire, and then they were gone. Harold's platoon moved up to the ladders.

Smyth-Woodford was standing behind them staring. Even in the deep gloom Harold could see his face was stiff with excitement. For him the great game was about to begin.

Sergeant Robertson walked down the line giving each man a slug of rum from a bottle he had purloined from somewhere. The silence grew around them and then into them. The waiting was terrible. Then came the sound that he was to come to dread. It was a mixture of a bark, a bang, and a rattle. It meant that one of the maxim machine gunners had spotted or heard something and had opened fire causing the flares to go up.

Other guns and a mortar joined in but the attackers were making a job of it for Harold could hear the deeper bangs as the Mills bombs were lobbed towards the trenches. The noise in the dark was even more unbearable than the silence. There were more bombs now and then the red flare for which they had all been waiting burst into the night sky.

"Up and at em men!" Smyth-Woodford's voice was more a scream than a shout for he was incapable of normal speech by this time.

The plan, as far as Smyth-Woodford understood it, was for front and reserve attackers to hold the German trenches while the artillery bombarded their reserve lines which then in turn would be ripe to be taken. It seemed simple enough to his innocent eyes.

They got through their own wire without incident and began advancing across no man's land at a steady trot. Harold began to feel the weight of his pack as they moved steadily uphill. Smyth-Woodford, who had no such burden, and who would not have noticed it anyhow had he been carrying every man's pack, moved out ahead of his troops waving his pistol in one hand and pointing a stick in the other. It was not until days later that Harold remembered how ridiculous he had looked. He was twenty yards ahead of his men and there was a danger of him losing touch even though from time to time he turned and gave some excited shout of encouragement. The weak moonlight made a mist of the night and it was only in the flickering flashes of the guns or the occasional glare of a flare that they could see him.

Then suddenly he stopped with a squawk of surprise. His stick was still pointed heroically towards the German lines but he himself had halted as though posing for a photograph. Harold trotted closer and saw that the officer had run into the German wire. Fortunately he had struck it near a stake and this had stopped his impetus from taking him beyond the first strands. He stood there startled with a tear in his immaculate coat. Then he pulled himself free and stood confused for a second. Sergeant Robertson rescued him. "To the right sir. The cutters have got through on the right."

The machine guns were silent as Harold moved through the gap in the wire though by now the 5.9s were lobbing their huge shells into no man's land. Instinct took over and Harold flung himself to the ground and began crawling towards the trenches.

The Germans sent up another cluster of sighter flares. Smyth-Woodford seemed to have forgotten that his platoon existed. The flares died out and as his men rose cautiously to their feet he started to jog trot on his own. Harold could hear him singing a house song from his public school. Then one of the German shells exploded within fifty yards of them and Smyth-Woodford fell with a scream as a piece of shrapnel sizzled into his flesh. Harold ran towards him. The officer was lying on his back clutching his stomach. His face was as white as snow and his smile was terrible as he looked up at Harold.

"Aaah Lawson. I'm alright thank you." Again the terrible smile as his teeth gleamed though a coating of blood. Harold saw that his hands were clutching his coat and then their strength gave out and the truth was revealed as the coat fell away and Smyth-Woodford's entrails writhed out like a bucket of worms. The young officer saw the horror in his face and gave a scream that was to cut into Harold's dreams for weeks, even when he had become casual with death.

Smyth-Woodford died before him. He had never seen anyone die like that, at such close range, in such an overwhelmingly intimate situation. He watched as the dead officer's entrails steamed into the cool night air.

For a moment Harold felt compelled to reach out and touch them but before he could do so Sergeant Robertson appeared standing over him. "Come on son, or you'll join him."

And then Harold ran onwards to the German trenches shouting horribly. The first wave had caught most of the defenders in their dug outs. Many of them had died when the attackers sent Mills bombs bobbling down the steps. The German dug outs were often deeper than those of the British, which gave them added protection against shelling but once caught in them there was no escape.

The Germans were sending reinforcements up from the reserve lines as Harold leapt into the front line trench. His arrival at the battle scene was far from heroic. His left foot landed on the leg of a dead man twisting his ankle. He rolled over near fainting with the pain. His stretch of trench had been cleared of Germans but about thirty yards away to Harold's right the trench cut away at forty five degrees to another section which appeared to be linked to the support lines.

A terrible battle was raging at this corner with both sides bombing and firing at each other from close range. One soldier panicked in the killing zone and climbed up to the lip of the trench. He was firing his Lee Enfield straight into the advancing Germans. He died in seconds as the spitting light from his gun made him an instant target.

Harold tried to move but he could put no weight at all on his foot. When he tried to raise himself he sweated with pain.

A stick bomb bobbled into the trench and exploded almost immediately. Harold clung to the earth and felt the body in front of him shudder as it took the shrapnel. He heard the screams of the others who did not have this protection and he squeezed himself to the ground.

He could hear the bullets zipping about him. It was terrible, like fighting blindfold. No one could survive this fury. A shell aimed at the German rear fell short and a whole section of trench just disappeared. The earth fell like rain about him. It seemed impossible that he was still alive but he was because he could feel the pain in his ankle. Amazingly the shell had saved his life because it had killed the nearest combatants, friend and foe alike. Men were falling all the time. Sometimes their screams were such that he could hear nothing else as they scalded the air. No one could stay here and live. The German reinforcements were arriving in droves by now. The counter attack was overwhelming. He dug his bayonet into the ground and pushed himself up on to his good foot He clung to the side of the trench and hopped along until his hands found a ladder. He pulled and hopped upwards until he was able to roll away into no man's land, crying out in pain as the ankle caught the ground. Then he started to crawl away as quickly as he could. He remembered the cut in the German wire and got through without incident as the retreat flares went up. He had not gone twenty yards when his comrades ran past him crouching like jockeys. One of the maxims started to fire into no man's land but most of the German guns seemed to have been knocked out. The bullets started to zip about him and he started to crawl frantically, not feeling the pain anymore. He discovered he still had his rifle. His hand hurt from gripping it.

He guessed he was at least six hundred yards from his lines and already the dark was falling into the dawn. His leg was throbbing again. Dawn was coming as sure as death and just as swift.

He began to shout for help. The maxim traversed the no man's land but still he shouted. He must have passed out and when he regained consciousness someone was dragging him over the ground. He felt something tear at his puttees and the soldier said, "That's the last of the wire." It was Sorrel.

The ambulance driver warned him that the road was bumpy and he clenched his teeth so as not to scream. He passed out again and when he woke up they had put a make-shift splint on his leg.

In hospital he was told that Selby and Bennett were both believed to be dead. A Jack Johnson had landed within yards of them and they had simply disappeared.

His father and mother hugged him in turn. They asked him about the war and he did not know how to reply; he was aware of the futility of even making an attempt. Instead he smiled and pointed to his leg. "I broke my ankle jumping into a trench. Some hero eh!"

His mother stared at him. Her face was white and tired. There were long silences especially during the day when he and his mother were left alone. A mood would sweep him out of doors and he would say as cheerfully as he could. "Well I'm just off for a walk." Thus he escaped into his thoughts.

Then one day she surprised him by announcing "I'll come with you." She had, he noticed, already rolled up some sandwiches in greaseproof paper and she carried a bottling jar full of milk. He thought no more of it even when she insisted that they walk to the old stones and the Holy

Place. It was as he remembered it, a scene of pagan beauty, possessing a strange, wild serenity that always arrested him. He noticed an empty jar on the largest stone and suddenly he knew the purpose of his mother's trip. He looked at her questioningly. "For Daniel?"

She nodded. "I come here each week. It's the least I can do."

"And the food goes. But who takes it?"

"He does."

He said nothing and she felt the need to elaborate. "I just know. That's all."

Harold felt tears welling up in his eyes. "I think of him often," he said. "Do you remember the arguments we had, how he attacked my 'world of concepts' as he called it and how he determined to live only with things that were near to him?"

Edith a smiled weakly at the memory. "I never heard the like. He left us a letter. He said that if the Germans invaded the village he would come to fight."

Harold saw the tears well up in her eyes and tried to rescue her. "He will too mum. To the death."

He hesitated before going on. "I want to tell you something about the war," he said. "It was after I broke my ankle and I was trying to get back to my lines. I called out for help. I was in great pain and one of the German machine gunners heard me and he began to rake no man's land. His gun jammed but he must have fired hundreds of rounds at me in a wild rage."

He watched as his mother gently placed the sandwiches and the milk on the largest stone. She picked up the empty jar and placed it in her large coat pocket. "Go on." She smiled.

"Well when I was lying in hospital I got to thinking about the German. We had never met of course, and never would but he could have lost friends that night, he probably saw some of them die and he wanted his revenge. As he tried to kill me I felt so close to him, a fellow traveller and for the first time I actually felt the meaning of Daniel. Do you understand?"

"You are brothers Harold. That is your link, your bond."

They spoke little on the walk back.

Already there was a strange yearning for him to get back to the war. The rest of the world seemed so unreal compared with it, yet so inviting that the temptation to remain frightened him.

So did Dominique. He could picture her clearly in his mind as she lay in the half light with her dark, damp hair coiled against the white of her skin.

When he first told her of Daniel's flight to the wild he had expected her scorn but her eyes lit with interest. She hardly spoke for an hour after that and her eyes were far away as though she was living in the vision of Daniel.

Jud refused to go for a drink at night.

"It's because of Daniel," Harold said at once.

Jud shrugged heavily so that his huge shoulders appeared at once both strong and tired.

Harold pursued him. "Has there been trouble?"

Jud hesitated and Edith jumped in to tell Harold about Willie Collins. She returned to her knitting. She looked as frail as porcelain but he could sense the inner strength in his mother still. "There's been feeling. That's all," she said.

The following morning he took his favourite road to the hills, past the tree where the hay wagon had stood on the day he and Daniel had argued a lifetime ago. He walked on and on without thinking until he found himself at the edge of the forest which stretched as a far as he could see to either side of him. He looked into the dark mass and shouted his brother's name. He knew that Daniel was not only surviving here but living. He began to walk along the fringe of the trees calling out to Daniel.

For a second he was tempted to walk into the forest to join his brother. In that moment he felt the inner life in his brother, the sense of joy he had experienced as they walked through the woods and across the streams; he heard their young voices, loud and careless. Then the moment was gone.

He shouted Daniel's name again and again but there was no reply. He knew that Daniel could not leave the forest just as he could not join him in it. They were both set on their paths, prisoners of circumstance, both learning their separate language of survival. For him the war beckoned and he had to return. He could not escape it for it held him with a weird chemistry of pride and terror.

16

Each morning Daniel walked over to one of the taller beech trees and clasped his arms round its trunk. His hands were just able to meet round the other side and he squeezed gently at first but with increasing pressure until his arms and shoulders ached. He felt the tree and the ground; he was part of this forest.

It was summer and he knew that he could survive the next few months. The winter was his only fear and it was a dominant one. Soon enough life would change; some would leave some would sleep and some would die. It was the way things were. To test himself he had gone three days without eating and was relieved to find he felt no serious upset.

In the first two months he had used only three of his precious tins and one of those was to reassure himself that they were keeping in their primitive storage place.

He had soon learned to kill but his first attempt had almost ended in disaster. He found a spot where the pheasants rested at night, about a mile from his shelter. He walked there early evening carrying a large stick and a haversack. He lay in the bushes and waited for the dark. Luck was with him at first. He was the only predator in the area and the birds did not bother to rest on the higher branches. He knew that pheasants, like most birds, woke at the slightest sound. He lay still on the cool earth as he watched them come to their trees. He lay for thirty minutes after the last bird arrived and then crawled out slowly from under the bushes sweeping his hands before him so that he could avoid snapping any twigs. He could see half a dozen birds standing on a branch of one tree. There was no wind so they were sleeping well out from the trunk, making them easier to spot.

He had been practising throwing a knife all week but that was in the light and at eye level. He stood up slowly and set his balance, legs apart as he picked out his victim. Then he let fly with all his strength. The knife struck the bird at the apex of its body severing its right leg. The pheasant fell crying to the ground and all the other birds were up in an instant calling to each other in alarm. The wounded bird called louder than any of them and Daniel caught a glimpse of it at the base of the tree. He ran forward with his stick raised seeking to end the dreadful sound. But the bird fluttered away so that the blow missed the head and broke a wing. He lost it in the dark until the pheasant cried out again. He ran towards the noise but his foot caught on a tree root and he crashed to the ground crying out at the searing pain in his ankle. Amidst it all he felt a lump beneath his chest and he realised he had fallen on to the bird. It lay warm, still and dead. He had broken its neck but the blood was still oozing from its wound soaking his trousers and shirt.

He lay there recovering his senses filled with a strange mixture of elation and desperation. His leg hurt too much for him to contemplate walking back to his shelter, and in any case he could not leave until he found his knife.

He pushed the bird from beneath him and pulled off his boot and sock. He could feel the swelling in his ankle but as far as he could judge it was merely a sprain. He wrapped the sock around his ankle but left the boot off. The cold got to him in the night. In the morning he felt stiff and hungry.

All he wanted to do was to limp back to his shelter and rest but he knew that he must retrieve his knife. He had had the foresight to mark out the tree on which the bird had been sleeping with his boot. He crawled around for a half an hour but there was no weapon. He was about to give up for that day when he remembered the bushes. He spotted the flattened ground where he had lain in wait for the pheasants and from there he traced his movements to the trees. Once at the spot where he had thrown the knife he found that everything fitted into place. He limped past the tree and then dropping to his hands and knees he made a careful sweep five yards to either side. After only a few minutes he saw the knife half hidden under a tree root. He limped home with the pheasant in his haversack. He could not afford to let it hang for a few days; he had no reserves of meat and he refused to break into his precious tins. So he ate well that night and for a couple of days after that. He used the bones to make stock for soup.

His main fear was that he had scared the birds to a new resting place or to the higher branches which would make it more difficult for him to catch them. He decided he couldn't afford another mistake so one afternoon he climbed about fifteen feet up on a beech tree and carved a target into the bark. He then attached a roll of string to the knife and began throwing it. It took only a few throws for him to realise that he had been lucky to hit the bird at all for only one of his first ten attempts hit the target. He practised for an hour a day for a week.

By now he was confident that he could kill or wound a bird with his first throw and he proved himself right that night. After that he raided the pheasants only once a week and used the rabbit traps as his main supply of meat. He began to find a great reward in his life. He was proud that he had demanded to live his life as he had seen it and had not been carried along by an unthinking wave of jingoism like so many others.

He had learned a new set of values: he could take nothing for granted; he fought and worked for each scrap of food, each square inch of cover, and each flame of warmth. To live was an achievement and that gave him a sense of pride in his life.

A sudden squall hit the forest one night in the early summer and he rose to discover that carelessness was punished in the wild. The rain had seeped through the badly lain tarpaulin on top of his supplies. Many of his matches were so badly soaked that the tops had been washed away from the wood. In a moment of inspiration he dipped the survivors in warm candle grease but it was obvious that his supply of matches would not last until the winter never mind through it. He decided that he must create his own fire. There and then he resolved not to eat until he had at least started on this task.

He started by using his hands to roll a stick into some wood shavings but achieved nothing more than a number of painful blisters.

After this he stuck four sturdy sticks into the ground and built two tiers of trellis into which he could position his pointed stick. He positioned the trellis over a large chunk of wood into which he had dug a cavity which was filled with wood shavings and dry grass. He cut a groove into the pointed stick and fitted a coil of greased string round it. He found that after a couple of adjustments he could hold the stick steady in the two trellises and that by pulling the string from one end to the other he could get his pointed stick to revolve at great speed. Within a minute the shavings smouldered and then broke into a hesitant flame. He quickly piled on some more grass and shavings and when this took he added some twigs and then some sticks and logs. It was done. He felt as though he had completed a painting. He used some logs to build a three sided wall around the fire to reflect the heat.

As time went on he learned to refine his fire building. He used shavings only from the soft wood of the fir trees and for his revolving sticks he selected only the hard wood of the beech tree. He learned to build up a fire from dry grass and shavings, to twigs and then to small branches which he shaved with small cuts.

For the first time he believed he could survive a winter. He knew too that eventually he might have to face another hazard. If the war started to become unpopular the soldiers would come looking for him. They would have to, to deter others.

With this in mind he spent the next two weeks building a hideaway. It took him two days to find a suitable beech tree. It was about one hundred feet tall and its first branch hung fifteen feet from the ground The second layer of branches were thick enough to support him and to hide him from the ground. He spent the next two days cutting wood into six-foot lengths. By now he found climbing easy and he quickly carried the branches up to the "second floor" as he called it where he lashed them together with lengths of greased string which he wound into a thin rope.

After two hours he had built a platform six feet by five secured tightly to the branches and to the trunk. He tried to imagine the tree, stark and naked in the winter. He guessed his hideaway would still be difficult to spot. The following day he took out about twenty tins from his food hole. He put them into his haversack and took them to his hideaway. He tied the tins together and secured them to the platform. He had learned the value of foresight and he spent the remainder of that afternoon trying to visualise the future threats he might face. He saw himself being hunted in the freezing cold, without shelter and leaving footprints in the snow.

He decided he must do two things immediately. The rabbit pelts which he had sewn together made a cover of about five feet by five. To this he sewed one of his woollen blankets leaving only a fist sized hole in a corner. Into this he stuffed pheasant feathers that he had saved. Each time the blanket bulged at the bottom he sewed another line across. He had only filled about half the cover when he ran out of feathers. However he estimated he would have more than enough to create at least two of these improvised covers before the winter.

His next task was to cut himself a one-foot pair of stilts which he could strap over his shoes. He made them out of wood and carved the outline of a fox's paw on each. He had no illusions that the prints would pass all but the most amateurish scrutiny but it would gave him a fighting chance until the snow covered his tracks.

A week after he had finished work on the tree he made a journey to the west road. He had not been walking more than half an hour when he came to a bank in the forest. It sloped steeply, up to six feet high in places and ran roughly parallel with the road.

He guessed it had once been some sort of defence dyke for people who had lived in the hills, people who had left hundreds of years ago allowing the trees to reclaim the high land.

He studied the ground carefully before returning to his shelter. The trees were in full bloom and the forest full of musty scent. The air was still and warm and he was sweating by the time he walked back to the dyke carrying a spade and a knife.

He cut a three foot square of turf from the broadest and steepest part of the dyke. The turf was about four inches deep, enough to contain the roots. He began to dig into the bank, piling the earth to his left The soil was fine and easy to move but by the time he had gone in a couple of feet he found it difficult to angle his spade so that he could shovel away the earth. He started to use a new tactic, spearing the spade into the earth, breaking up the soil which he then swept away with his hands. He stripped himself in the heat and worked his way slowly but methodically into the bank. The deeper he went the harder it became and by the time he had gone in four feet he was panting with effort. His sweat had turned the dirt on him into slime and he had to use some of his drinking water to wash himself down that evening. The next morning he took a small axe and a hand spade with him. Before he started digging he cut some wood supports for the sides and the roof. It took him an hour to get these into place and then he crawled into the hole and began hacking away with his spade once more. He was soon covered in dirt but was so determined to carry on that he hardly noticed the state he was in. Every six inches he placed more sticks for support. By late afternoon he had tunnelled eight feet into the bank. He was exhausted and sore from working in such a cramped position He brought up a third of his tins and stored them in the deepest part of his burrow.

Finally he bound together a grid of sticks and sewed them to the piece of turf he had cut away at the opening of the tunnel. He placed this over the entrance and leaned back on his spade to survey his work. He could do no more. If they caught him now it was because he could not avoid them or through some misfortune.

He scattered the pile of loose soil. He had two lines of refuge now, one to the north and the other to the south in addition to his temporary sleeping places that were scattered over a square mile of forest. He was content. He could concentrate on the day to day struggle for life, like everything else in the forest.

17

Sorrel was gone. At six o'clock each morning the barrage opened up and Harold remembered that Sorrel was dead. One of the Jack Johnsons had caught him with a direct hit on his dug out. When they pulled him clear the smell of burned flesh from a wound in his chest was almost a relief. There had been no slow suffocation as each breath merely sucked more dirt into your nostrils and throat.

Death had come in a flash and that was as much as anyone could ask. But at six o'clock each morning the Germans opened up with their barrage for fifteen minutes and Harold remembered him.

All of his friends were dead now so there was no one left to hurt him. It was true that Dalby still lapped around him like a dog doing tricks. Harold rejected him abruptly but it made no difference. Dalby recognised him as a superior being with a kind heart and clung with simple faith to the one thing that he believed in: Harold was destined to survive this war as would those who were shrewd enough to stay near him.

Suddenly the firing stopped and Harold told himself that he was still alive. They left the dug outs and lined up at the firing steps on alert. He looked along the ragged line in the trench and for an instant he imagined that he was standing in a queue for death. They were all hopelessly bound together from the cynical veterans to the innocent rookies like the blond-haired Saunders to whom Harold gave one bit of advice each day.

Today he told him: "Don't dwell at crossroads." Saunders had blinked uncomprehendingly and Harold had added: "Artillery targets."

Breakfast came but the pale sausages only satisfied Dalby's appetite for complaint. They could smell the bacon from Lieutenant Bellamy's dug out and Dalby snarled in his strong Glaswegian accent; "I'll kill the fucker one day."

As if in explanation his sausage fell limply off his fork. Harold turned wearily away before Dalby launched into a new torrent of abuse. He was tired and stiff from crouching during the barrage. The grey morning light made his eyes itch. He spent his turn on the fire step looking out across the bleak no man's land through a periscope. Patches of the defence wire and much of the communication wires had been blown away by shells. That meant a wiring party in the night. He sighed. His shift at the front was up. He would be relieved in the afternoon. His horizon for that day was to survive it. Everyone seemed to have the same idea for there had been a tacit truce in that part of the line for weeks. It was rumoured that one of their wiring parties had actually exchanged greetings with a Hun patrol a week ago, though Harold doubted the story.

Still, as Dalby pointed out, the morning barrages had been the only act of aggression for some time now. The only irritations were the lice, the giant black rats that fed on the dead, the smell of bodies in shallow graves, and the stench from the latrines. "Quite nice really." Dalby spat in parody of a tough guy. Saunders had looked at him in awe.

There was the usual rush back through the reserve lines that evening even though there was no firing from the snipers. The jostling and swearing with the unfortunates on their way to the front was almost obligatory.

Back in the village they were allowed to wash in deep barrels of cold water and were given clean uniforms Harold heated his bayonet in a fire and began popping the "iron crosses" in the seams of his jacket. The lice would be back of course but he looked upon it as a sign that he was still alive, that he still cared about his body. Some of the men laughed at his aversion to lice. They'd lived with them all their lives. For Harold though it was one last line of defence. He had even shaved his head to discourage them.

In the morning he woke to the sound of birds through the flimsy wooden walls of his hut. The smell of warm urine hung heavy over young Clements's bunk. Harold wondered how many patriotic doctors had conspired to pass such a youth fit.

They spent the morning charging and screaming at suspended sandbags while a Sergeant Major bawled in contempt at their puny efforts, especially when an officer was in hearing range.

"Someone ought to tell the twat we never use the fucking bayonet." Dalby wiped the sweat from his head with the sleeve of his tunic.

Harold shrugged. He and all the others knew that such protests were useless. The bayonet covered three feet in front of you. The Mauser sighted at six hundred yards and in any case no one but a fool would use a bayonet when their rifle could kill at ten times the range. And as for close combat this was mainly fought out with bombs. Some platoons carried them in canvas buckets. However the army was convinced of the value of their traditional weapon. And the artists liked it.

There was bad news in the afternoon. They were told they were being moved out. As they marched to the station Harold was reminded that he was living in two worlds. The lush green fields were sawn through with the dusty tracks of the transport vehicles leading past the sagging walls of a farmhouse hit in the last advance.

They climbed aboard cattle wagons. Harold sat in silence allowing the chatter to go on round him. Someone was whistling out of tune. Harold tried to stop thinking but he couldn't. Bennett, Sorrel, Selby and the others were threatening to invade his conscious again so he thought about the war.

He remembered using a German helmet to barter for eggs with a French peasant woman. He'd put a bullet through it before he set out and her broad face beamed as he stuck a finger through the hole. "Un moment." She traipsed along a rutted track and into a tumbledown wooden barn. Two minutes later she reappeared with some eggs scooped into her apron. The woman laid out them on the dry ground and then took the helmet from him. She filled the helmet to its brim with eggs. "C'est juste." She nodded eagerly.

"C'est juste," he smiled. He took off his own helmet and put the eggs inside. There was room for some more eggs but the peasant woman just cackled when he pointed this out to her. She walked with him to the gate gabbling away too quickly for him to pick up a word but he got her message.

He saw the Germans as the enemy and as such he respected them as being brave and organised. To underestimate them was potentially fatal. It was an important objective assessment. To her they were vermin.

The rumble of the cattle truck brought him away from his daydream. Then he escaped again into his thoughts.

It seemed to Harold that when things went dramatically wrong in the world no one questioned their own actions and beliefs; they merely sunk deeper into bigotry. Daniel had argued this very point to him. He'd seen further than any of them.

This war would not end in victory but in exhaustion and in that state new ideas would flourish until the whole process was repeated.

But there had never been war like this one where two enemies had slaughtered each other at such close quarters for so long under such similar conditions that every man, even the dimmest of them, must realise that the reality was that they were one, bound by their common suffering and humanity; that they had to break free as human beings of the restraining dogmas on which their tired old societies rested.

He could see Mr Ormsby shaking his head at such thoughts. "Silly socialism," he would say. "And it'll end up as corrupt as everything else."

Perhaps his former employer was right but Harold could not abandon the hope that man eventually would be capable of making a mental leap so that he could see reason. He refused to accept that all the greed, intrigue, and politics of the world could prevent man from aspiring to common sense eventually. Surely people would eventually see beyond the myopia of nationalism and embrace instead philosophies. The world was getting smaller each year and Harold believed people must adopt some new way of thinking or become involved in some great catastrophe.

He smiled at himself, very much aware that his brother Daniel would nod in approval at such thoughts.

When they reached their station there was a crowd of wounded waiting to be put on the train. One of them watched Harold's platoon clamber down from the trucks and shouted: "More cattle for the slaughter."

Dalby glared across at the man on crutches. "Hop it mate. Fucking hop it."

Dalby's comrades laughed, delighted that the tables should be turned on these men who had got a Blighty.

"Yeah," the soldier leaned on his crutches and sneered. "I'll think of you when I'm back home."

"Aye and perhaps I'll walk over to you and have a chat next time I'm on leave." Dalby grinned as his platoon laughed again.

"IF you get home." The soldier on crutches grinned at this crucial point.

"Oh I'll get back. I'm going to shoot off a toe tonight." He looked pointedly at the one-legged man. "You must be a fucking awful shot."

"Fuck off!" The one-legged man shouted cheerfully.

Dalby contented himself with a broad wink and then walked away.

They billeted in a dark church hall and then were moved through the bustling town of Albert the following day. The traffic on the roads hampered their march and they eventually rested in a dusty village four miles to the north east.

After four hours they were moved to a field filled with rows of tents. Harold and his platoon were quick to appreciate the luxury. It was warm enough for them to leave the tent flaps open overnight. The noise of the traffic kept them awake.

Harold had never seen so much activity. Troops were moving past all the time, some on horse-drawn carts, some on lorries, some on buses, but most of them marching in files.

The big push was coming. Everyone knew that now and it seemed impossible that anything could withstand the onslaught of so many men and machines.

Harold's' platoon was moved a week later. He sat on top of a London bus that still had its number. "Jesus," someone said. "I used to ride on this back home."

Rogers laughed, "Well what are you complaining about. At least this time it's free." Everyone laughed to take the edge off their nerves.

For the first mile there was nothing to suggest there was a war apart from the soldiers. Then they came across the odd shell mark. A church steeple had been blown away, by one of the 5.9s, Harold guessed. The village had been evacuated.

The bus stopped a mile short of the reserve trenches.

There were a few shell holes but they had weeds in them so Harold assumed the Germans must have turned their guns on other targets.

The officers urged the men forward. They did not have to carry the sixty -six pound packs that the trench troops bore.

Soon they were moving up through the support trenches but there was still no sound of gunfire. They moved through a link trench and then another and at last they were at the front. The dark, earth walls zig zagged along the bottom of a rise. The German trenches, Harold judged, were about seven hundred yards away. As usual they had retreated to the high land, following the ridge so that the distance between the two lines of trenches differed by up to one hundred yards.

They spent four days in the front line, standing to at dawn and dusk. The silence was off putting. They all knew it could not last. They were moved back to the second line and then the third before being given a few days off in the village. It was called Fricourt, Harold was told by one of the peasant field workers. This village had also been evacuated though this must have happened within the week because Rogers found a huge ham in one of the cottages. They boiled it for supper and ate it with some apples taken from a nearby orchard.

The silence had begun to affect their nerves and each time they returned to the front they jostled and pushed each other to get to the dug outs after they had raced sweating through the support lines with their packs weighing them down. Everyone knew that the big battle was about to begin.

18

As Edith knelt in her grotto she felt shame and anger in equal measure.

Pebbles dug into her knees through her long dark dress. Her eyes, pinched closed, were scalded with tears and her body shook with sobbing.

For once the light summer breeze sighing through the leafy trees and the cool water bubbling its way downstream could not soothe her. All she could hear were the echoes of the Reverend Martin as he boomed with sulphuric certainty from his pulpit on the equation between Love of God and Love of Country.

There were mighty battles ahead, he told the congregation and when those mighty battles had ended, as indeed they must, there would be a day of reckoning for those who had fought like Christian soldiers and those who had not.

The latticework of red veins glowed on his nose as he recalled the strange boy who had stared at him as though he was staring through him. He paused for dramatic effect and his eyes held Edith's until she looked away and her body shook with her crying. He did not speak as she rose to her feet and walked a tired walk up the aisle and out of the church. The door closed and the heavy iron bar snapped down on the sneck. As its last echo died away the vicar looked round his congregation. "These are harsh times and we must be strong." His voice rang out once more.

Edith consoled herself that she was in her own church now. There were no stone walls, no icons, and no echoes in a dusty, musty air. Here everything was of nature and she felt the echo of men from another age. She left a brief note to her son. She was afraid; she knew that the world of her village was moving on but she didn't know where. She left some flowers and food before rising slowly to walk to her home and to her husband.

The Reverend Martin was man who instinctively found comfort in belief...belief in God, belief in his country and belief in the establishment. Yet even he, as he flicked his rod by the side of the river and sent the bait flashing out into the rock shadows, was moved to a moment of compassion at the memory of Edith's sunken figure. She was he thought, a simple woman who had no idea of the concepts or implications of the war. And yet she had become a victim of it.

He flicked the rod again and the line hissed out over the water. It was inevitable that there would be casualties in war; that was its nature; they were necessary sacrifices for good to prevail. These were his thoughts and he felt no alarm as he saw the huge figure of Jud Lawson approaching.

He left his rod on a forked stick as he rose to acknowledge the farmer.

"Afternoon Mr Lawson. I do hope your wife has recovered."

Jud had been rehearsing a speech all the way down to the village and he would not, could not, deviate now. "I aint an educated man like yourself vicar. And I aint particularly religious either."

The vicar nodded.

Jud's voice grew stronger with conviction. "But there's one thing I do know. To do what you did to my wife this morning. That wasn't Christian. And it wasn't manly."

The Reverend Martin sighed one of his best sighs. "I meant her no harm Mr Lawson."

"No harm!"

"There was an important message to get across. What would you have me do, Not speak out because your wife was in the congregation."

Jud looked at the vicar and for the first time saw him as a man and not as an icon. "You spoke to her not to the congregation. What was so important that you would destroy a decent, honest woman vicar?"

"That was not my intent Jud. The country is in mortal peril. We need every fighting man we can get."

Jud looked at the vicar for a few seconds and then spoke in a quiet voice. "That's as may be vicar but who are you to make the call. A man who destroys people who trust you from your pulpit and then goes fishing in the afternoon."

He turned sharply and was gone before the vicar could recover from his shock at the words.

The only voice Daniel had heard in months was his own. Yet he missed no one, he was too busy fighting to live his life. He had dared to stand apart and though he did not find satisfaction or conceit from this alone he was proud that he had tackled and overcome the unknown. It gave him a great sense of being alive. There was still so much to do and always would be as far as he could see.

Throughout the summer he took the end off his shelter and woke with the light. But the winter was always in his mind. It was the last unknown and he tried to anticipate every possibility. He ran barefoot through the forest; he climbed trees as though he had been born in them. He had the ease of a natural athlete and that summer there was not a man in the county who could have outrun him or outfought him in the forest.

He had learned to trap the pheasants with a line of nooses as they flew to their branches for sleep.

He fished too with half a dozen baited hooks laid on a line across a dark section of the river. At night he plundered the fields for potatoes, carrots and Swedes. He had planted some of the potatoes in a rich stretch of land near the river bank and stored the rest.

Every second day he travelled to the edge of the forest to lay and clear the rabbit traps among the elder and ragwort bushes. He moved slowly and cautiously. There was never a time when at least one of his twenty snares did not have a victim.

It was on one of these trips that he became aware that he had a rival for the territory. Two of his snares had been uprooted on consecutive visits and, a week later, when it happened for the third time he examined the trap carefully.

The noose had been pulled so hard that the wooden supports were broken and the wire had gone. Surely no rabbit had the strength to do this, even when filled with the deepest panic.

He got to his knees and, with his hands gently tracing over the ground, examined the area round the trap with great care. About a yard from the trap he found traces of blood and a small tuft of rabbit fur shivering in the turf. He began to look for prints but there had been no rain for days and he soon realised the task was hopeless. But the more he thought about it the more probable it was that a fox had moved into his territory. It was just conceivable that a big buck rabbit might break free from badly-laid trap, but not three times in succession. There was not room for himself and the fox so that afternoon he packed his knife and some food in a haversack and trotted over to the burrows. He was sure that the fox must have come from the north because his traps to the south of his shelter had not been touched.

He moved quietly to the edge of the forest taking care to stay down wind of the fox's likely route. He cut some small twigs and laid them over a pile of loose grass at a couple of the rabbit burrows. Then he set up a couple of traps at the entrance to the escape burrows on the other side of a hillock.

There was a light breeze and he wasted two or three matches at each hole before he got the fires going. He had not long to wait before half a dozen rabbits fled the burrows in terror and one was held helplessly in a noose, He killed it with a quick flick of the neck. Killing did not offend him. He had a countryman's experience of death. He had seen his first pig killed when he was five. John Meredith had brought the heavy axe down through the skull of the screaming pig which had keeled over legs still kicking.

He removed the smouldering fire before any of the other rabbits became trapped. He did not need them and he had disciplined himself against wasteful killing. He took the dead rabbit and hung it one of his traps on their running routes. Then he ate his food, laid out his knife and settled down to wait. Dusk came quickly, the night air was warm, the moon nearly full and the sky clear and full of summer.

As he lay on the turf he amused himself with the thought that he was at war. Not only was he fighting a daily battle for survival but here he was fighting for territory against an enemy. He wondered whether the fox might be alarmed by the smell of smoke. . He knew that at worst it would only be a temporary deterrent for eventually hunger would overtake its sense of caution.

Then something broke his thoughts; there as no sound but he knew his enemy was near. He reached for his knife with his right hand and felt for a makeshift club with his left.

The memory of his first pheasant was still with him. He reasoned he could not hope to kill a fox with one throw of his knife so he planned to hit it on the shoulder or the back of the thigh to slow it down and then finish it off with his club. He lay there hearing only the silence. The moon was at his back but he could see nothing. Then one of the dark shapes he had taken to be a bush moved slowly. It must have stood there for a minute without moving and it alarmed him that he had not seen it; that he was still learning; that there were things in the forest that could move with greater stealth than he. The fox showed dark grey as it moved out into the moonlight.

It stopped still sniffing the air and then moved forward with a low growl towards the rabbit. As it pulled at the carcass Daniel rose to his knees and hurled the knife with practised power but the fox sensed him and in that instant swung to face him snarling in fright. The knife missed the right shoulder and grazed the left instead. The fox called out in pain and then fled into the forest. Daniel saw it limping but knew that he could not catch it.

There was one hope; that it would leave a trail of blood.

He wanted to see the matter through to the end now; so much so that if the fox did escape him he hoped it would return eventually. He was warm enough in the night air and he decided to sleep out until the morning. The excitement of the night kept him awake for a while but when he did sleep it was deep in the clean night air. He woke at first light and walked across to the rabbit. He found the knife in a couple of minutes and then looked for blood.

He slowly followed the path the fox had taken into the forest. For the first few yards there was nothing and then he saw a smear of blood against the trunk of a tree. This gave him hope because the fox must have been in pain and fear to have brushed against a tree. He began to move in semi circular sweeps all the time heading north. He had gone twenty or thirty feet before he spotted the second patch of blood. It was much smaller than the first and he knew then that his task was hopeless. He walked further into the forest for a few minutes and then stopped.

There was nothing to do but to go on as before and wait

for the fox to return as he knew it would.

For the first time since he had come to the forest he felt defeat. He carried the rabbit home to his shelter and gutted and skinned it. He opened his food store and took out a tin of bully beef. It was a change, a feast, and it tasted delicious with a mashed potato and a chunk of boiled turnip.

The following day he cut off the back legs of the rabbit and put them in the smaller of his two pots with some potatoes and carrots. He made his way three hundred yards into the forest and built a small fire over which he constructed a roof of branches and leaves to filter the smoke.

Daniel poked a stick into the pot. The rabbit meat had turned from a silvery red into a grey brown colour and his stomach persuaded his head that the meat was almost ready.

He laid out a tin plate and lay back staring into the speckled sky from the floor of the forest. The earth was dry and warm. He wore no boots he wanted to save them for the winter. Back in his shelter the rabbit skin lay stretched on a wooden frame. Life and death were everywhere, in every minute and every inch. That was the same in the forest as it was outside, but here, he felt closer to it. The rabbit that he was about to eat had stared at him from the trap, its eyes somewhere between terror and death. Daniel looked around the clearing. The beech trees were seventy feet tall, with great dark mushrooming branches. He had made himself build his fires away from his home so that if they were spotted he could still escape any would-be pursuer. He had trained himself to be conscious of soldiers since an incident of two months ago. He had visited his mother's place of worship in the glade about a mile from his camp and there his eyes had caught a blue enamel jar filled with field roses standing on one of the stones. The flowers were dead and the small package of sandwiches and meat lay curled and decayed. Under the jar his mother had pinned a note but the writing was almost indecipherable. He wondered how many times it had been soaked and then dried by the change in the weather. He could not read a word of her letter but he felt a message of love from her little gesture. After that incident he returned to the glade once a week. He had no writing materials so he stuck his thumb in the mud and left a print on the battered slip of paper his mother had left and stuck it under the jar. There was nothing for three weeks and then he saw the roses again. This time they were fresh and pink. The bread was soft and warm and the cheese had not begun to sweat. He guessed he had missed his mother by a day. He did not want to see her or rather for her to see him like this. His hair was lank and long and he had taken to growing a beard. He still washed every day but he knew he had changed; that his skin had hardened and that he looked older than his years. He wanted her to remember him as he had been. Her note told him that three of the villagers had been killed in the trenches and that she feared for him because some of the miners resented him. She feared the soldiers. They had been through the village on a recruitment drive two weeks ago and she knew some of the villagers would have told his tale to the soldiers. Her note ended by telling him that Harold was well and went on. "One day, I know, they will come for you. Your loving mother."

He cut off a lock of his hair, washed it in the stream and placed it in the jar amid the wild roses.

The smell of the rabbit brought him away from his thoughts. He stuck a fork into the pot again and examined the meat. It was done. He plucked the legs from the pot, heaped them with vegetables and gnawed away. There was great pleasure in simple food when it satisfied a deep hunger.

19

Before every attack Harold wrote to Dominique and his parents. He tried to keep each letter chatty and cheerful because there was no point in alarming them with the truth, and even if he had tried he was sure it would not get past the censor. Also he found a strange comfort in indulging himself in the illusion. There were times when it almost seduced him.

On this occasion however there was no need to lie about the mood in the trenches. The men were confident and hopeful. Everyone believed that the fate of the war would soon be in their own hands.

Harold did not add that he had long ago disciplined himself to discount such hopes just as he had refused to make new friends to take the place of those who had died. Friends were only one more way in which he could be hurt. He had taught himself to live from day to day and by any standards he had become an expert in survival. With one glance he could read any terrain, note possible sniper points, or pinpoint the areas most likely to be raked by machine guns. And the sounds; he knew them as well, the different shells, the different guns, the tap on the wire posts at night.

He knew best of all that, despite his expertise, there was a huge area of providence which determined whether he lived or died and over which he had no control. He had a better chance than most of surviving but most of all he needed luck.

He did not despair at this knowledge. If anything it made him more determined than ever to tread the narrow path of survival between death and his sense of duty.

He took out his buff pay book and turned to the section for his will. It was blank. He had refused to write a word in it. He kept it in his breast pocket. He'd always believed that if he did get shot it would be through the heart.

The British guns opened up and no one had heard anything like it; not even the veterans as thousands of shells sought out the Germans in their dug outs. For mile upon mile along the front line the white hot metal gouged its way into the earth seeking out its trembling prey.

Harold was resting in the village when the barrage began and he knew just how the Germans must be feeling. It gave him great heart. The shelling went on for day after day until there was hardly a soldier who did not believe that they were wasting their shells for surely no one could survive such a barrage. Yet still the guns fired on an on until at last one evening they were assembled in a huge three-sided rectangle in rank upon rank. A general rode up and down on a white horse telling them that they were to take part in a great battle that was to end the war. The horse kept trotting this way and that so that some of what he said was heard but some of it was lost. He told them that they would be able to walk across the no man's land but it was vital that every man obeyed orders. Any failure to do so would not be tolerated. He held them all in an icy glare and there were some who muttered in resentment at his words. They'd been up and over more than once, and all had lost mates. And where had the old man been? Sitting in his chateau, thirty miles back. They knew he'd leave the horse and take a limousine back to headquarters. Then it would be time for dinner and time to look at some maps.

Everyone was given a dose of rum that night except those unfortunate soldiers whose companies were run by abstinence men. There the soldiers had either to go without or to barter with more fortunate comrades. They moved up at dawn. A major sat astride his motionless horse watching them assemble in the village square. The guns still rumbled on, all but drowning the scud of boot's on the cobblestones. The man behind Harold began to cough. Harold could smell the last cigarette on his breath.

The Major's role was to stay in the village and oversee the support troops but the sight of the men so moved him that he raised his sword towards the red of the dawn light so that it glinted on the steel.

He shouted: "Soon the sky will be red with the blood of our enemy."

Some of the men began to laugh at this. They believed

that the Germans were dead already. The image of the officer flicked a switch in Harold's subconscious so that he saw almost in the same instant the statue of some heroic cavalry officer at home and then Smyth-Woodford pointing his baton as he dangled on the wire. A food hamper had arrived from his mother the next day. It was stamped with a Fortnum and Mason label. It sat there for a week after his death. No one touched it and then one night the men realised that a rat had gnawed its way through the wicker. They threw out the hamper in disgust over the trench in no man's land where like its owner it dangled on the wire. The Germans shot it to pieces over the next few days. He remembered the warm, sweet, pungent smell of apricots as they decayed in their broken jars.

Harold poured his rum into one of his water flasks. He had long ago learned to improvise on what he carried in his pack, assessing that at least half his equipment was useless in most given circumstances. He always carried two bottles of water since he'd heard the cries of the dying in shell holes. In addition he always carried two hundred rounds in a bandolier and most important of all, his trenching tool which he invariably stuck at the top of his pack.

As they moved up Dalby walked beside him. His face was grey with nerves. Harold had seen the look many times before. It was the face of a man worn down with living so long so close to death. Eventually these men stopped fighting and accepted, even welcomed their end, for that was the only escape. And once they'd lost the fight to live they invariably died. Dalby, he knew, was nearing that state. He was losing the anger that sustained him and with it the energy that made him think and act quickly. The evil in him was reaching for a state of grace.

The barrage went on for another day and then, just after dawn, they set off the mines. A huge mushroom of earth was thrown up and the whole world seemed to shake with fury. Someone to Harold's right became so alarmed that he braced his foot against the rear of his trench for he could feel the earth moving. He broke a leg but no one heard his screams.

Another boy, he looked fifteen at the most, lost his nerve amid the terrible thunder of the mines. Harold could see his mouth open and, from the terrible tightness in his face and the panic in his eyes, he knew the lad was crying in terror as he moved away. Someone flung out an arm to stop him but the boy had the strength of fear and he brushed past without a falter in his stride. Harold lost sight of him as the boy pushed his way through the packed rows of troops.

Seconds later a whistle sounded and the first wave of soldiers began to clamber up the ladders and over the top.

Harold always tried to be one of the first to go because he reasoned it gave him the best chance of getting past the sighting points of the Maxims before they opened fire. They threaded through their own barbed wire, their rifles trailing butt first to the ground. They had been told not to charge because it was feared they'd be exhausted before they reached the German lines. Immediately ahead the ground lay brown and baked in the summer sun. A rabbit zigzagged across them but there was no way back for it. The lines of Khaki stretched along the trenches for as far as you could see like a vast line of beaters at a shoot. As Harold trotted forward he became increasingly alarmed. This was not as it was meant to be, not as they had been told it would be. Firstly the German barbed wire was till intact and further on he saw hundreds of grey lumps which he knew must be unexploded shells. He had got thirty, perhaps forty yards through his own wire when the Maxims opened up. He ducked as low as possible and started to run towards the German lines keeping clear of the mass of advancing troops who he knew would attract the main fire. Behind him the massed lines stopped as though in shock that they were under fire and then whole swathes of them began to fall. Dalby moved up alongside Harold his face open in terror. He was beyond thinking for himself now but his instinct told him to stay with the man he knew to be the mentor of his platoon. Harold would know what to do, how to stay alive. A soldier in front of them began to shout curses; his high pitched voice cut through all the other noises. Then he spun backwards. Harold ran determinedly up to him and stopped in astonishment as he looked down. There amid the carnage, amid the thousands of soldiers dying on this morning was a man from his village. He could hear Dalby screaming but he stood in shock looking down at Larry Collins who was clutching his shoulder. He stood there for seconds, unable to move. Then he reached down and pulled a water bottle from the wounded man's pack. He placed it in Larry's good hand and smiled. The world was moving slowly and he could smell the earth and he saw Larry and then his village and then his home.

"It's you Larry," he said at last.

The wounded man stared at him from the ground. "Don't stand there Harry. Get yourself on or you'll get shot."

Harold gave a ragged laugh. This was proof that the world was mad. That he should meet Larry Collins and that Larry should lie injured and warn him that he might get hurt.

Dalby was pulling hard on his arm. "Come on you stupid bastard," he snarled.

"You'll be alright," he told Larry and then started to laugh again because what he saying was so preposterous in the circumstances.

The barbed wire was all round them, as thick as his little finger and feet deep. He looked desperately for a way through. There was none. A dud shell lay feet away and he began to curse. He could hear the bullets zipping about him, spitting up the earth. No one was going to get within fifty yards of the trenches. To his right he could see a machine gun mounted behind a concrete slab. He ran forward a few strides and hurled a mills bomb with all his strength. In his panic he must have held on to the bomb for too long for it exploded in mid air. The gun went quiet. Some of the Germans were so excited that they left the cover of their trenches and began shooting wildly into the ranks of the British. Twenty or so of his comrades had tried to get through the wire. They hung with the weight of the dead, dangling men on the heavy wire, jerking occasionally as another bullet pierced their unfeeling flesh. Harold stared in horror as they danced their death dance on the wire.

He fired his Lee Enfield at one of the Germans then he himself was hit. He went down. He felt no pain, not at first, as he lay on the ground wondering whether he was dead or dying. He felt a sudden remorse. He had not written to Daniel.

Dalby stopped a few yards from him like a horse waiting for a tug on its reins. Without Harold he could not go on. Harold began to crawl towards a shell hole. Dalby stared at him and then walked slowly towards him. He reached down for a grip on Harold bandolier and began pulling him.

Harold's leg was agony now. Every pull from Dalby was torture. He could take no more. As they trailed past Larry Collins he grabbed on to the soldier's leg. The weight was too much for Dalby now and he began to curse. "Leave the fucker." Then his head disappeared. The body stood for a second like a boy refusing to accept the umpire's decision and then it tumbled mercifully away from Harold and on to the lip of a shell hole.

Harold could hear the warm blood pumping from the stump that had been his neck. Collins started to vomit. The effort put weight onto his injured arm and he screamed with pain. The sound woke Harold from his nightmare. He reached out and pulled Collins with one arm. "Come on. Or we're dead." He motioned with his head towards the shell hole. Harold lay on his back and pushed with his good leg. His face was grey with pain. "Come on tough guy."

Collins grinned and moved up alongside him. It took them ten minutes to roll into the hole. Then Harold fainted. The sun was burning him when he recovered consciousness. The right leg of his uniform was crusted with blood. He rolled over gingerly. There was a hole at the back of his leg. The bleeding there had stopped too. He looked across the shell hole. Collins was lying on his back. Harold thought he might be dead and then he heard gentle snoring. Dalby was still dead though, hanging over the rim. He could see the raw stump sticking out like butchers meat. He wondered what had happened to the head, the face. He reached out for his rum bottle and trickled some of its contents on to his wound. He felt as though he was branding himself but he had seen enough cases of gangrene to endure the self inflicted torture.

He sipped gently at a water bottle. He wondered whether he could endure the pain and climb to the rim of the shell hole to collect Danby's bottle. It seemed ironic when he considered how many bodies the little Scotsman had looted in his time. He usually had half a dozen watches strapped around each arm. How futile that seemed now He decided to collect the water on the way back to his lines.

Collins gave a groan from across the shell hole. He had not spoken for an hour. Harold saw a bubble of blood come through his lips. The big man's face was grey. He needed treatment but Harold knew it was suicide to venture out into no man's land. He could hear the mortars, the Maxims and the Mausers and the bark of the Lee Enfields. He guessed there must be scores of wounded men sniping at the Germans.

He wondered whether the whole attack had failed and realised that he didn't much care. He had a nice neat wound that would take him home if it didn't get infected and provided he could make it back to his lines that night.

He heard Collins's voice. "I believed them. I fucking believed them." He sounded tired and spoke in a monotone. "They said all the Germans would be dead."

Harold laughed. "Yeah, well they would say that wouldn't they."

Collins began to cough a deep hacking cough. Then he dozed off again. Harold looked at him with new concern. He couldn't leave him and he couldn't move him. Not before nightfall. The bullets were still fizzing overhead. Every so often the stump that had been Dalby gave a jerk and another piece of him came away. They were shooting at everything they could see. He lay on his back. A butterfly danced above him. He stared at it and started to laugh. An afternoon at Selby's came into his mind. He'd lain out on the long lawn lazing in front of the great house thinking how grand it was; how proud he was to be English. Where was patriotism now? Probably in the chateaux thirty miles behind the lines where the generals moved things on maps and those things became men who ran breast-first into machine guns in wave after wave; all to die and not know why. There would be more arrows on maps after today and more men would die and if victory didn't come some new platitude would have to be invented to disguise the awful truth of the dangling bodies on German wires that grew like bramble unbroken and untouched. They'd advanced with great gallantry… not a man had taken a step back… heavy casualties inflicted on the enemy…a major enemy assault prevented at Verdun. He knew the way their minds worked now and knew there would be thousands yet to die until the vile stench of the mountains of dead rolled like slow fog to the generals. And then it might stop. He looked across at Collins and recognised a strange, nobility in the simple man, and he remembered his own innocence; his belief that the war would forge his character.

It had not done that. It had crippled his emotions. No matter what he faced back home he would look back and say: "It was worse there. It was worse there." He would make it a buffer between himself and anything that might beset him in the future. "It was worse there." That was all he needed to say. How could anything else disturb him when set against this awful reality?

He remembered the morning and seeing his comrades go down in waves; sight of their faces, so open in shock, haunted him. They were like boys who had been led to believe in something, and then suddenly, in one mocking moment they'd had that belief taken away. And then they'd died.

Yes that had been the look in their eyes, just before they died. They'd been told that Germans would all be dead. But they weren't. They'd been told that the wire would be destroyed. But it wasn't.

There was a terrible anger in him. He knew he would never let this day leave his mind; he would recall it every day for the rest of his life; at the start of each day he would erect it like a monument and for the rest of that day he would go out into the world and try to change it. He would not, could not forget it. The men in the chateaux must go. Their day had been and gone, and so had that of the ladies who stuck white feathers on the breasts of boys, the fresh-faced officers who went off to war and told each other what a great game it all was. They must go too, though most of them had gone already; either they were dead or, like him, they had changed beyond recognition. But the fathers remained thirty miles away as did the people who schooled them and the institutions that had inspired this monstrous lie of jingoism. They remained and they must be made to go.

If there was one justification for all this it had nothing to do with this absurd carnage, or even the reasons that lay behind it. It was that the world must change because of this war A generation had been betrayed and now there must be a turning point, a reference point in history where people could see that all those who died out here, all the young lives who had been taken before they were tired of life, had not died for nothing, but that their deaths had caused the biggest social change in history.

If he lived one more day or twenty thousand more days he would never abandon these men. He was tired but one more thought invaded his mind. It was that the men of both sides who had been forced to fight this fight, had more in common with each other than mere nationality could give them. If they had so much in common in death surely they must have so much in common in life. How could they be enemies? They were all caught in the same trap and were killing each other to survive. That was the irony. He tipped his rum bottle to his mouth and drank until he could not get his breath. Soon he would be drunk and able to rest.

He thought of Dominique. Was this what she had seen in him? She could have chosen anyone and yet she had taken to him at their first meeting. Once he had asked her why and she'd whispered one word. "Excitement." He slipped away overwhelmed by the drink, the wound, and the exhaustion. It was dusk when he came to and the battle was still going on. Against the light of the sky line he saw a rat as big as a cat gnawing at Dalby's stump. He raised his Lee Enfield, shot it, and was pleased by the sound of its exploding flesh. Collins was shaken by the sudden explosion so near him. "Christ!" He shouted. Harold grinned.

"It's almost time to go tough guy."

Collins scowled but he like Harold knew that their only hope of survival was to crawl back in the dark through no man's land. They could hear the Mausers and the mortars going again and Harold guessed that many of the British wounded had tried to make it back instead of waiting for darkness. Perhaps they could not wait. Perhaps they could feel the life slipping out of them and instead of blissful exhaustion they were filled with panic because they so wanted to live.

Harold had the nerve to wait until it was absolutely dark because that would give him the best chance of living and he wanted to live more then he had ever wanted to live. It would truly be absurd for him to survive the madness of the advance only to be shot crawling back to his own lines.

The shells started coming over again. From instinct he grabbed his trenching tool and began to dig into shell hole. The work tired him quickly and he gave up after a few minutes. But the hole he had created was large enough for him to put in his head. At least that part of him would remain. Death would not have the dreadful anonymity that had been Dalby's fate. He lay there and fell asleep. When he woke his head was no longer lying in the hole but it was dark.

The Germans were still firing, and though there were many who were tired and sickened by the slaughter there were still some who had lost friends to the snipers or the shells who were grimly shooting it out. He knew that the time had come for him to risk his life again.

"Larry!" He called across to Collins in a low voice.

"Yeah," Collins nodded. He rolled over on to his good shoulder and began pushing with both legs. Harold could hear him grunting with effort. Harold laid his helmet under his injured thigh and held on to it with his left hand in an attempt to make a primitive sledge. He told himself that pain was mainly in the imagination though as he moved over the lip of the shell hole it seemed very real.

He felt the earth change shape as he got on to the flat ground. Collins was grunting ahead of him and Dalby lay stiff by his side. He could hear the ticking of his watches. He waited for the flicker of one of the big guns and saw the body a yard to his right. He reached out and felt the cold stiffness of the man who had saved his life because he could not save his own. He could not bring himself to take Dalby's water bottle though never had a dead man needed it less.

He called across to Collins who grunted in reply. They began to push their way back to the lines. After twenty minutes his thigh was throbbing and his shirt was soaked with sweat. Collins called to him. He was on the right and some distance ahead. Harold wondered whether they were going round in circles. He leaned up on an elbow and looked ahead of him. The darkness was impenetrable and then a gun flashed and he could clearly see the mounds of English dead. He waited for ten minutes and then started to push again. Something pulled at his tunic; it was a dead man's hand. He shuddered and pushed on like a boat through rocks.

"Larry." He called out. Collins replied. He was closer this time. Harold crawled towards him. The moon came out briefly from behind thick clouds and he saw the death white in his comrade's face. Blood had dribbled in a black line from his mouth. Collins turned and his black eyes found Harold's.

"How far?"

"The worst is over Larry."

In front of them someone started to scream, a long, loud, high-pitched sound that rose to a higher pitch at each scream until Harold wanted to shoot the man to make him stop. The terrible sound prompted them to push on again, this time side by side.

Harold pushed on harder this time, cursing at each stab of pain but learning to live with it minute by minute. He estimated that he was moving half a yard with each push and he began to count so that he might rest every fifty yards.

He had gone one hundred and thirty seven yards when he heard Collins call out. "I canna go on Harold. I just canna."

Harold stopped by him. He could see in the moonlight that Collins's shirt was stained with new blood.

They lay together in silence and then Collins whispered. "You go on Harold. Bring help."

Harold shook his head. "No."

"It's for the best man."

"They won't find you."

One of the guns flickered into the night air.

"What's to do then?"

"We'll do it together." He gripped Collins's tunic on his right side. "Hold my helmet under my leg." Collins did as he was asked. "Right." Harold's voice sounded unduly loud in the dark silence. "Now when I say one we push with our feet." As they pushed on Harold began to realise how incredible it was that he was still alive. Surely only the dead could have got nearer to the German lines.

He looked into the blackness of the sky and as he moved onward he was faced with a new horror. Someone was screaming again, to his right this time, and then he pushed into another body. He moved to the left to be confronted by another body and another to the left of that. He steeled himself and pushed over the nearest corpse. He heard Collins gasp in revulsion as he was faced with this new horror. There were other bodies and more beyond them. Harold panicked, not feeling the pain in his leg now as he struggled desperately over hands, legs, trunks and heads of his former comrades.

His right hand was wheeling out like a man swimming the backstroke as his body writhed over the sea of dead, and then worst of all, his clutching fingers caught one dead man in the eyes. The touch of them would remain with him forever. They were as cold and stiff as a fish's eyes he had felt as a boy. He made one final convulsive effort and with the strength of the mad hauled Collins over this last obstacle. Suddenly he could feel the cool freshness of a patch of grass. If it had survived in no man's land so could he.

He wiped his hands sure that they must be caked in blood and held back the bile mounting in his throat. He moved on pulling Collins who was all but inert. He could feel rubble underneath him and then the rim of a shell hole. He moved carefully round this new obstacle and about twenty feet further up came up against the barbed wire that defended the British lines. The guns flickered again and he could see the bodies at the wire, see the flapping bits of tape at the exit points. This was one of the gaps where they had queued. The bodies lay thickest here. He felt the thrill of a reprieved man.

"Larry! We've done it."

Collins answered him with a low groan.

His elation was short lived. His exhausted body leaned against the wire setting off one of the improvised alarms. A Lewis gun started spraying into No man's Land. He shouted for the fool to stop but no one could hear. The panic spread. The British must have been fearing a counter attack and some Lee Enfields joined the Lewis gun The Germans started to return fire. Harold clung to the ground tearing his nails into the earth.

The weight on his thigh was agonising. He jerked up with the pain of it and then there was sudden oblivion. One of the Lewis guns hit him in the forehead. The bullet drove splinters of bone and brain before it, pushing their resistance into a tight mass that in turn gave way, driving a deeper wedge until the bullet passed out the back of his head leaving a fist sized hole. He fell face up and when they pulled him in in the morning there was just this little hole in his forehead that disturbed the peace in his face. They found Larry Collins too. He was staring at Harold. The wound reminded him off an apple he'd raided from an orchard. A worm had wriggled in through the ripe skin.

Five hundred miles away Daniel swung his axe into a log. The blade hit a deep knot that sent a shiver up the wooden shaft. Daniel felt a sudden tremor pass through him and stood shaking in shock as he called out his brother's name.

20

Edith Lawson saw the postman approach in his slow deliberate way and felt a nudge of alarm as he turned right and cycled up the rutted track towards her door. She noted the bulging bag and the weary stoop to him.

She called to Jud. As she opened the door he stood behind her. Edith could feel herself fading as Jack Robson handed her the buff telegram. Jud shone with pallor as he moved beside her.

The postman stared at the couple. He stood halfway between coming and going and not knowing how to move on. Edith's face was stiff with grief. "I suppose I'd better open it," she said at last.

"It would be best." Jack nodded.

She tore off the top, stared at it and then handed it to Jud.

Jack stared at the pair of them. "I'm sorry," he said. "God missus! I'm so sorry."

He looked at them again. They were staring hopelessly at the telegram. He got on his bike and rode to the gate. When he looked back they were still standing at the door.

Edith felt Jud's warm arm wrap round her shoulder and chest. She stood staring down the lane at the retreating figure of the postman. Her eyes were so dry they hurt when she blinked. She willed herself to weep but she couldn't summon the tears. She heard her own voice saying; "We'd best be leaving a note for Daniel."

In the past Jud had greeted her faith in the Holy Place with gentle amusement but today he simply said: "I'd like to walk with you."

She turned and smiled into his face and he kissed her on the forehead.

Jack Robson had no need to pedal for the last half mile to the village for the slope pulled him down. The next telegram went to the Turnbulls, and then to Watsons, and then the Mooneys and then the Smiths and then the Forsythes, and then the Johnsons, the Normans, the Rices, the Irwins until there was hardly a house in Milford that had not received a telegram and the Rowlands received two for both their sons had gone to the war. Each message said that a son had been killed or was missing. The Milford, Swannell and Upper Valley Pals were no more; they had been shot to pieces in one bloody morning.

As Jack Robson rode heavily from the village along the river road Milford knew that her sons would never return to the fields and the pits and Jack Robson fought back his tears as he picked up speed chased by a ghost load of memories.

He remembered Mrs. Mooney screaming "Oh NO! There must be some mistake." But there was no mistake. He remembered his own throat aching as he sobbed with the villagers so that by the time he got halfway through the village he could not speak; he could only hand out the telegrams and watch. He remembered the fluttering of the curtains as the village woke to his presence. He remembered looking down the main street and seeing the villagers, men and women he had known for thirty years, standing like condemned people at their doors. These were things that he would never forget unless they were drowned by more horrors. He felt for the buff envelopes in his bag. There were two more villages on his round.

There were no more flags and bands in Milford that war. The recruiting officers stayed away. The villagers were not even allowed individual grief. Their own tragedy gnawed at them and when they looked outside for comfort they saw only people locked in the same suffering.

There was no cure except time and so they waited. Some looked for someone or something to blame and remembered Daniel. They hated him because he had become an outsider and as such was an easy focus for their anger. Why had he been allowed to avoid the danger? Why had he been allowed to avoid his duty?

Some, if they had seen Daniel would have reported him to the army camp that had been set up near Swannell.

However Daniel's cause was helped throughout by two staunch allies, Susan and Old Willum.

Susan knew that Daniel was not a coward though she could not understand why that was so important to the men. She did not know why Daniel had left the village for the hills and the forest but she did know that he had a spiralling soul that seemed to her more compelling than any of the accusations against him.

She sensed he saw and felt things that others did not. She had wisdom of instinct beyond many of those more articulate than she. But her voice alone would not have made much difference; she was only a young girl, and though she was regarded as honest and decent in the small community, she did not have the sway of Old Willum who, since Bill Moffitt had died earlier in the year, had become the oldest man in the valley, who could convey more with a spit into the fire at the George than most men could by jawing on for five minutes.

In the street, or on the rare occasions when he walked the lanes, there was not a man or woman who did not stop to have a word with him, or mention to their kin that they had done so.

"Daniel thought in a way that few of us are blessed with. That's all," he said one night at the George before sitting by the fire and sucking on his pipe. He raised a challenging eyebrow. It hovered briefly over a bloodshot eye before coming down to rest like a tiny fox tail. No one spoke, for few of them understood what he meant.

Only Willie Collins felt strongly enough to argue with the sage of the village but months ago Old Willum quelled him by asking: "And do think a coward would dare to fight that lad of yours you are always boasting about?"

Old Willum watched Willie struggle for words and then, in an act of execution, picked up his beer and walked to the window that faced the valley towards the hills.

The trees hid the Lawson's cottage but he looked beyond to the great beech forest on the high land. The others followed him to the window so that they all looked up the slope in silence and then someone asked:" Do you think he'll stay there through the winter, Willum?" There was a murmur from the rest of them for this was a question they had all been asking.

"Aye," said another. "If he stays up there through the winter then perhaps some will believe you more

165

readily Willum."

Old Willum stayed staring until some thought that he must not have heard them. Then he turned slowly to them sucking on his pipe. "Oh aye. He'll stay there. This village might not see him again. Or his like."

He stared at them thinking how similar the men looked in their flat caps, their dark waistcoats and their collarless shirts. He held Daniel against the lot of them. The way the lad glowed with life did an old man good, especially when he had seen little above commonsense in others.

They were at opposite ends of their lives but both viewed the war as a bloody invasion. Without it he could have taught the lad all the ways of the country; he could have taught him the history of the fields, and in return? He was in awe of the boy's natural knowledge; his ability to be near things. He remembered Daniel as a boy of ten looking at a swooping swallow as though he was flying with the bird. The life they could have shared would never be now, and that was that.

Larry Collins returned from the hospital that autumn but he was not the same man. He would never hew the coal again. His right arm was gone and the sleeve of his dark jacket was neatly pinned at the shoulder, a sight that had become all too common.

Willie attempted to celebrate the return of his son but the boy refused to go to the George. "Give me some time dad," he said in a flat voice. The laughter had gone from him and he brooded, not like his father in drink, but like a man trying to ease the bruise on his soul. For weeks he would not talk about the war and no one dared to ask.

Eventually he was coaxed into the odd drink at the George but no longer did he seek the centre stage. He sat like an old man against the wall staring into his drink.

His father had never spoken to his son of his fight with Jud but he had never forgotten it. He told himself and anyone who would listen, that he had been in drink and Jud had taken him unawares.

He was a fighting man with a puncher's chance against anybody. The bruise to his pride lasted long after the bruise to his face had disappeared and to him the Lawsons were as one. Five pints into the night he began to brood. He looked out of the pub window, saw the hills and said: When the snow comes we'll sharp see little Danny down from the hills."

Larry got up from chair and, without looking at his father, said in a loud voice. "Good luck to him. He was the only one of us who knew what he was doing." The shock waves of that sentence went through the pub and through the village the next day. Not only had Larry defended the lad who'd run to the hills but he'd taken his side against his father.

More was to come as Larry stared into the room with a maverick look in his eyes.

For the next few seconds he was the old Larry, ready to fight over a sandwich and there was not a man in the room who did not note the flash of anger. His left arm pulled at his empty sleeve.

"You want to know about the war," he shouted. "Well I'll tell you."

He drank so quickly at his beer that some of it spilled on to his shirt.

He told them about the agonies of trench feet, about doctors sending men back as malingerers, about a friend who'd drowned in mud when he fell off a duckboard, about another who'd smothered in a dug out when it collapsed under shell fire, about the lice, about festering wounds, about the green bile that spewed from men caught in the gas, about the thousands ordered to make futile charges at machine guns, about the stiffening cold in the winter and the stench of bodies in the summer, about the rats as big as cats and about the terrible sound of the shelling that went on for hour after hour until men clung to the ground in their dug outs and screamed for no more but still the shells sought them. He told them of the generals who lived in chateaux thirty miles away working on their maps. "They lied and lied and lied," he said. "They told us no one would survive the barrage. They told us that the wire would be blown to pieces, and when it was all proved wrong they said the plan was to wear down the enemy. So why did they have cavalry units ready to charge through the broken lines eh?" No one answered. "They lied and lied," he said. "So I say Good Luck to Daniel. For a start his brother saved my life. His brother was a hero. Not me. It was he who dragged me through no man's land when I'd given up with this." He pointed to the flap at his shoulder. "He was as bad hurt as I and when I couldn't go on he refused to leave me. He refused to save himself. So don't no man go calling him or his family in front of me. He died saving me but he'll get no medal. And why? Because he was shot by his own side. But he was bravest man I ever met. So I say Good Luck to his brother Daniel!" He drank the last of his glass, slammed it on to the table and walked out.

Larry didn't speak the following day or the day after that. The doctor spoke of the need for rest.

On the third day he left his breakfast untouched. He stood up from the table. "Me coat ma please."

His mother did as she was bid slipping the right sleeve inside the buttons.

Willie stared up from the table. "What's up son? Where you going?"

Larry turned at the door. "To the Lawsons. I needs must make my peace."

And with that he strode out into damp autumn air.

He walked through the village failing to acknowledge nods and greetings of those he passed. It was only when Edith opened her door that he spoke. Edith stared at the pale-faced young man. She was conscious of the history of the two families but felt no apprehension as she looked at the young man's tear-filled eyes.

But when he spoke his voice was strong. "I've come to tell you about Harold." His voice began to falter. "He saved me. He was the bravest man I ever met and I'm truly sorry it was him who died and not me." His tears were teeming down his cheeks now and she felt them drip warm on to her neck as he collapsed into her arms.

21

A bunch of wild roses fluttered fitfully on the flat stone that weighed down the letter from his mother. The note was protected by a torn piece of canvas. Daniel knew the content before he tore it open. He read the short message quickly with tears scalding his eyes.

That afternoon he gathered some stones and placed them in the form of a cross. On the largest stone, which stood at the apex he scratched a crude 'H'.

He looked to the sky. The low sun lay in a red smudge on the hills and he knew with the certainty of instinct that though his brother's body might lie in France his spirit resided here with the souls of men and women down the ages who had felt compelled to pray to a greater being in this mystical grove.

He felt the faint sun, heard the trickle of the stream and the whisper of the wind through the low branches.

As he prayed he felt the common bond with all of those who had been here before; all who had sought to make absolution or to make supplication; he felt the presence of his mother and was aware of the quiet shuffle of her bell skirt as she knelt; and he heard the laughter of his brother as they had played on the rocks and stones years ago. It was, he decided, a place for poets.

The summer had passed hot and sad; the crops were picked, cut, mown, stacked, and were gone from the land in which they had grown. The birds fled and the rains added a damp chill to the air. As the leaves fell to the sodden earth and in time became part of the earth there were many who looked up to the hills and thought of Daniel.

There were some who openly supported him now. More of the wounded came back to the village in dribs and drabs and for the most they had the same tale to tell as had Larry Collins; they wanted rid of the conflict and waited for it to end as a man waits for a sickness in him to end.

The villagers did not know why Daniel had gone into the hills. Many thought he must be a pacifist but nevertheless he became a symbol of the resentment that the village now bore towards the war. There were however some who still believed that the only way the war could end was for a still fiercer and determined assault. But even among them the fairer minded looked up to the hills and wondered whether Daniel could survive the winter or whether he would come down and admit defeat. If he left the forest for whatever reason he was a lost man to all who knew him.

It was thus that Daniel's name became linked with the anti war sentiment that grew in certain parts. One of the newspapers mentioned him in an article on pacifists and deserters and called him "the wild man of the woods". By the time the winter came Daniel had not been seen by anyone for eight months but had become known throughout the valley. As his fame grew many a lonely shepherd was mistaken for him and his name was spoken from Morpeth in the south up past Milford and north of Alnwick.

The Government introduced conscription later that year for the losses of the army had been so great they could no longer be replaced by volunteers alone.

The authorities began to fear Daniel's fame and they tried to seek him out. However the only policemen in those parts were Andy Lamprey who was based at Swannell and the relief man who was sent down from Alnwick every second Saturday. They both had to cycle miles each time they were sent on a search and were in a foul mood by the time they reached Milford to spend the afternoon crashing about in the forest. Only the odd poacher had occasion to rue their visits.

As the weeks moved on and winter closed in Daniel could think of little but his own survival. By now he had made two great blankets stuffed with pheasant feathers and padded with rabbit skin. He had also dug another deep hole into which he stored his wood. He tried to use the fire for cooking only because he feared someone would spot the smoke. But as the frost bit in, as the ground became hard, and as the leaves fell from the trees allowing the freezing wind to sweep through the forest he was forced to relent.

Some nights when the cold seeped into his bones he built the fire right by the shelter and piled it up so that it was still smouldering at dawn. Then, as the cold got worse, he was forced to move the fire into the entrance of the shelter itself. He built a three sided trellis to reflect the heat.

The first snow came but the slush that followed was worse. It soaked the forest and turned into ice at night. He caught a chill as the ground became as hard as stone.

For the first two days it was as much as he could do to keep the fire alight from the spare wood and to eat his meals from the cans. For the rest of the time he lay sweating and panting under the blankets. His shirt and trousers clung to him and his skin became soft and spongy so that he could wipe the dirt away with a rub of his hand.

Each night he forced himself to throw wood on to the fire shivering and aching as he went. If it had rained he would have died. If he had not been so fit and strong he would have died. As it was he lay for five days with no strength, knowing that he was nearer death than he had even been. He was not afraid. He had killed to survive and he accepted death as part of the life he had chosen.

It was this choice that he had made that had given him a broader insight into life. It was this that made him fight for life, not because he feared death but because life had become so vital to him. The pride in himself and in the life that he had chosen burned through him. He could not go back. At last he had something in which he believed, something to fight for.

On the fifth day he was through the worst. He moved more easily, the shivering had gone and he could stretch out from his shelter. Many of the trees were bare now and the snow had swept down the hillside. The white coating was as smooth as icing save for one ruffled track where a rabbit had run for shelter. A low, winter sun came out that afternoon and the tree shadows chased him through the forest. In the extreme of winter everything seemed black and white. As soon as he could walk he visited the rabbit traps nearest to his shelter. There was nothing. The fox was back. One of the wires had been broken and the snow was disturbed over a wide area. He scouted around until he found some spots of blood. They were dry and black. Here away from frenetic action round the traps he found the prominent pads of the predator. He tried to follow the tracks because he knew that foxes often buried their prey, but after stalking the trail a mile up hill the snow became patchy and he lost all trace of his enemy. He resolved to hunt it down. He was too weak at that moment but in a week or so he could start again by trying to work out the likely lairs in the area, or he could lay a trap with food again and wait for the fox to come to him. He knew the fox must be killed even if it took weeks of work. There was not room enough for both of them in the forest in the winter.

He had by now adapted himself to life in the hills as best he could. His clothes even his spare footwear came from rabbit hide. He had cut himself a bow and fashioned some arrows using the melted tin cans to form tips. The beech wood did not make the best of bows but his greased string was adequate and he learned the difficult art of honing his arrow shafts straight enough to keep on course.

He greased the shafts with animal fat and found that after a couple of weeks he could hit a tree at fifty paces. However the arrows rarely penetrated the tough bark for the tin was too soft a metal.

Every morning he packed the blankets into the largest of his haversacks and stored them in different hideaways. He carried his bow and his knife everywhere now. The fox had made that imperative. As a precaution against attempts to hunt him down he had stored a pan and basic cooking and eating utensils at each of his hideaways.

He found his boots a problem in the snow, his socks were threadbare and once his boots became damp they froze his feet until they hurt and then the boots took days to dry. He eventually found a compromise by sewing rabbit skins over his boots. He found that together they kept out the damp and cold on most days.

As soon as the trees were bare it was obvious that his loft was plainly visible to anyone who looked up from a radius of ten yards. It was too big a risk so he spent half of one day climbing up and down to retrieve tins and utensils. He left a couple of items of food and an old knife hoping to fool anyone who found them that he still used it as a shelter.

The only food he caught that week was a rook He put an arrow through one of its wings and dived on it as it hopped around screaming in fear and pain. Mercifully the weight of his body broke its neck but the bird's claws still raked his chest.

The meat was so bitter it brought up bile from his stomach. Only the breast and the legs were edible. These he boiled until the flesh fell of the bones. The meat tasted like wet paper. He made a thin vegetable soup from the stock and broke the flesh into that. There was enough to last him for three days.

He began to plan his defences. Over a period of two weeks he built three other primitive shelters two or three miles apart. He wanted them to be found so that his hunters could not conclude that he was living in the vicinity of any shelter they might find. Then he built fires near each shelter and scattered animal bones in the ashes. He was gratified to note that even the fiercest of his fires did not attract any attention. He took to sleeping in the shelters and by the fires. They were far away from his food supplies which were his real Achilles heel.

The fox came back. He didn't see it but the beast began to raid his snares once more. He waited until the next fall of snow and followed its tracks eastward from the rabbit warrens through the woods. He lost the trail again on the higher land where snow fell more frequently covering the tracks. He was running zig zag through the trees trying to pick up the trail again when he heard the terrible sound of screaming.

There was no doubt that it was from a man as were the others that followed it. His first instinct was to drop quickly behind a tree but as the noises continued at regular frequency he was drawn to them. He moved at a crouch two hundred yards or so towards the edge of the forest where the trees thinned sufficiently for him to see out on to the moor land.

There he was confronted by an amazing sight. Rows of man-like figures hung from a line of gallows faced by rank after rank of soldiers.

In between the gallows and the soldiers stood a small man who emitted a huge scream every few seconds. What he was shouting Daniel could not discern but he watched in fascination as the small man's body convulsed with the effort and at each scream the front rank of soldiers would run forward screaming hoarsely themselves as they stuck a bayonet into the hanging dummies.

The little man then raised his right arm and screamed again, at which the next rank of soldiers ran screaming towards the dummies. This happened time after time and if any soldier did not charge quickly, did not scream loudly, or did not thrust or disengage his bayonet with the expected expertise the whole rank was made to repeat the exercise until the little man was satisfied that every one of them had got it right

These were the first human beings Daniel had seen in months and he watched them half fearful until dusk when they were marched away down the hill. So the war was still on and his enemy was nearer to him than he had ever dreamed. After this experience he visited the edge of the forest every day to watch the soldiers. He made a habit of rising early each morning and trotting the two miles. He arrived as fresh as when he had started.

Towards the end of January the soldiers were assembled an hour earlier than normal at their camp. An early fall of sleet slaked across the space that they used as a square. The young officer ignored the biting wind, even when it cut into his neck as he addressed his men. He told them that they were to have one final exercise before they went to France and he was confident that every one of them would relish the task. He told them of Daniel and how he had ignored the call of his country while others had sacrificed their lives so that England could remain free. There was a slight murmur from the ranks and he realised he had not picked the right day to extol England's virtues.

"This man has been living in the forest," he pointed his arm towards the hills. "The police have tried and failed to track him down so now it has fallen on us to do just that. Men," he said. "I know you will not let the fifth down. If he's up there we'll get the bastard."

There was another murmur from the ranks and the young officer thought there was something exciting and fundamental about a hunt. "It will be a tricky job but there are extra rations of rum if we find him." This last promise sent a ripple of interest through the ranks.

As Daniel watched them marching up the slope he knew immediately that something was wrong. He watched as they spread out in a long line of one man to every ten paces.

They marched steadily towards the trees. The forest was a mile wide at that point and he knew that they would cut down south in a long line for four miles until they came to the west road. He had no doubt that more troops would be waiting to trap him there. The men at the west road were the guns and the troops could see were the beaters.

It took him a mere twenty minutes to jog back to his shelter he picked up his haversack and cooking utensils and ran towards his burrow in the dyke. He had at least an hour's start on the beaters. He had lived through this situation in his mind many times and he had a drill that at least matched the discipline of the soldiers.

His tins and blankets weighed him down at each stride but he was strong and fit. He kept to the rise of the land avoiding any patches of snow. When he reached his burrow he pulled back the opening and flung in the contents of his haversack. Then he strapped the haversack to his shoulders once more, pushed back the cover to the burrow and ran back towards his shelter. This time he collected as many tins as the haversack could hold and stuffed some candles into his coat pockets. He thought he could hear the soldiers but he could not be sure. The sound real or imagined gave him wings as he bent beneath the weight of his tins. By the time he reached the burrow for the second time he was taking in great heaving gasps of air and his body steamed as he took off his coat. He stumbled into the burrow and closed the entrance.

It was almost black. There were two pencil holes of light from the air holes fraying the darkness but that was all. He felt inside his coat for his matches and lit a candle.

That autumn he had tested how long a candle lasted in the burrow before it burned his air. He had counted at an even speed inserting the word 'and' between each figure and then had divided the total by sixty. He estimated that the air holes driven thinly through the dyke wall gave him just over three hours.

As he sat waiting for the soldiers he realised that he had not thought of every aspect of sitting inside the burrow. He had to fight off the severe temptation to look outside to see where the soldiers were. He tried to look through the narrow tunnels of the air holes but they had no breadth of vision He knew he could do nothing until the dusk. He began to ask himself what he would do after the soldiers had swept over him in a long line He presumed they would sweep across the road and continue their search. He hoped so for one of his diversionary lairs was in that area. They would not give up their hunt for him. He was certain of that.

The first of the candles started to flicker as it neared the stump. He used the last of the flame to light another candle and stood it in the soft wax. Then he gathered the rest of the grease and placed it in a small tin. He used a twig to push a length of string down the centre of the soft wax to form a crude substitute candle. It might work it might not. He had to try to conserve everything now. He placed the warm tin in a corner to cool. After another hour the flame began to make the air stale. He squashed the candle wick between finger and thumb and once more lay in the blackness. He took out his knife and began scratching at the soil until he had widened the bore hole like an archer's slit in a castle. This gave him more light in the burrow and a wider angle of vision outside. Still there was no one. Surely he was the quarry. He could not be wrong. He had considered the situation all that summer. In times of tension everyone feared the outsider. He almost pitied them their primitive dogmas. It was they, not he, who were the victims. They were locked in a prison of the need to believe that was so strong that they would not and could not accept any challenge to it. And so they ploughed deeper and deeper into ignorance.

And yet he was the one who was being hunted because he threatened them. He knew now the basic choice he had made. He had rejected the opportunity of self advancement, which over the years, could have given him power and influence, because it was servitude set against the alternative which he had chosen, which was to live his life to his own values and deal with the consequences of his need for freedom as best he could. It was far from perfect but, to him, less futile.

He could hear the soldiers now. They were calling for him and then suddenly a shot rang out. Then another and another. He could hear their shouts of excitement; he could hear their footsteps rumbling on the ground. He stared intently through the spy holes but saw no one.

The noise of the soldiers got louder and then it reached

a climax and rolled away. Still he could see no one but he knew they were gone. He had survived. He had beaten them. He was exhausted. He fell asleep.

He had no means of knowing how long he had lain there but when he awoke there was still a thin light from the bore holes and he could hear the soldiers once more.

He crawled to his spy hole. Still nothing. However he did not need his eyes to work out what had happened. The troops would have swept right down to the west road where he assumed they had met with another line of soldiers. No one could have crossed the road unseen so instead of marching south across the road they'd turned back. So the hides built for them to find had all been in vain. There could be only two reasons for them to turn back. He had been spotted in the vicinity which was unlikely, or they had found his real shelter and some food.

He lay there listening to the sounds of them shouting and crashing clumsily through the forest. It was worse than before. The tension of going through the whole thing again just as he thought he had survived was unfair. The noise seemed to go on for minutes though it could only have been seconds. He discovered that he had crawled away from the spy hole and that he was curled up tight, knees against his chest. He uncoiled himself and tried to regain his composure in the silence. He lay there with relief blotting out all else in his mind. During his life in the wild he had trained himself to expect the worst. He wrapped himself in his blankets and lay in his burrow until the morning.

He emerged like a rabbit from his burrow, cautious and timid. His eyes blinked in the bright light and it took him a couple of minutes to get his bearings.

A cold breeze thrust through the mighty trees. He left his blankets, his haversack, his tools and his tins in the burrow for he needed to be as mobile as possible in case he was challenged. He doubted that any soldiers remained in the woods. They would have had to light fires to survive the night and this alone would advertise their presence.

He listened for any sound of them. There was none so he began to trot back in the direction of his shelter.

He had not gone one hundred yards before he found the fox, shot through the chest, its white incisors gleamed in an open mouth and the dead eyes stared in final defeat. A couple of the beech trees had their bark blasted away. The soldiers had obviously been amusing themselves.

He ran quickly and quietly in a wide loop to his shelter. He approached from downwind. The heavy acrid smell of smoke invaded his lungs before he saw the carpet of ash and the rotting stumps. He also became aware of the warm smell of urine.

His food store had been disturbed. They'd taken the tins and defecated on the tarpaulin ground sheets and in his water store. Ironically his tree hideaway was still intact. Their line of approach had meant that their view of it would have been obstructed by two young beeches which were still heavy with leaves.

He climbed the tree and collected the tools which he had left to be discovered. Everything counted now. He was filled with an increasing numbness as he scouted through the woods.

Their prints were everywhere as they had walked heavy footed and careless through the bare ground of the forest. It was as though they had wanted him to know of their invasion, that they had gone through his domain with ease and would do so again if the fancy took them. They'd smashed two of his other temporary shelters and trampled on a tiny rose bush his mother had left him and which he'd planted in a small clearing.

He could almost feel their jeering and their sneering, their resentment, their contempt for an outsider that had turned to hatred as they had failed to detect him, as their excitement at the hunt had become a boring forced march through cold countryside.

How jubilant they would be if they knew how much they had wounded him. They had won though they didn't know it and would never know it. Even with the demise of the fox his chances of survival off the land was now minimal.

He had the tins left in his burrow, but half his matches had gone, the dry kindle and starting sticks had been soaked in urine and most of his tools had been taken or broken.

An explosion of anger took hold of him. Let them come to the forest every day he would not give into to them. He could hunt better than anyone, not like the gentlefolk with their beaters and rows of guns but like the trackers of old. He could move quickly and he could hear sounds that others could not. He knew the plants and the birds and the animals and the trees; the smell of the rain and the lick of the sun. He knew the warm places and the watering places. He could defeat them. He would defeat them.

But even was these thoughts rushed through him on a raft of rage he knew he was beaten. As he sat warming himself by the embers of his shelter he knew that he hadn't time to build a new home and hunt for food. Not in the cold. Not without his big axe. He found himself throwing loose sticks and broken branches on the fire of his home. The blaze warmed his body and to a lesser extent his spirits.

He sat there for some time, numb with doubt, and then was overwhelmed by a need to pray. He would go to the grove; perhaps his mother would have left a note for him. Whether she had or had not he would still kneel there and pray in this holy church of nature just as the men who had built the dyke had done before the time of stone churches. He imagined that they like him so many times before had prayed for a harvest or for success in hunting. He was back in their time and he felt the warmth of their company as he walked to the grove. He moved carelessly now for he knew that the soldiers had gone; they were men of the city and he would have heard their sounds. He was alone, even the fox had gone thanks to the soldiers. He laughed to think how insignificant it had been and yet while it had been the only thing of any significance it had dominated his thoughts. He could hear the water chuckling through the grove before he saw it. He hesitated at the edge of the trees before stepping into the clearing.

Even in the winter when many of the trees were stark and bare it held its air of serene calm. He lifted up his mother's stone and picked up a small envelope on which his name was written in her neat looped writing. It said: "Go to the west point of this place."

He looked along the trickling stream past, the slabs of flat stones and over the smooth rounded rocks and pebbles to a fringe of asp and alder trees. He could see nothing as he walked along a rough path that had been half flattened by feet.

He followed the trail into the trees and stopped at the sight before him. Someone had cut a little grotto out of the trees and round its perimeter stood a row of makeshift memorials made out of flat stones. Each one bore a name and a date of birth and a date of death and each date of death bore the date 1916.

There was one exception. The stone for Larry Collins had only a date of birth. At the foot of his stone lay a pair of shiny black boots. A short note was tucked in one of them. It said: "Hope they fit."

He looked around the stones. By each gravestone there lay a bunch of ferns or moss or beech leaves and under each of these the village folk had placed gifts of food tins, tarpaulins, rough blankets, trenching tools, tin cups, some tea leaves, some sugar. He felt his eyes salt with tears as he looked about the Grotto. His mother had laid a stone for Harold and under some withered wild roses he saw the glint of his father's axe. The Grove behind him held the footprints of man down the ages, hidden by time, but nevertheless he could feel the spirit of their common yearnings when he stood where they had stood. But here in this little clearing, here was something new a bond between himself and the people of his village. He looked up. The winter sun lay blood red in the sky. Soon the winter would be over.